I

ha

Copyright © 2006 by Dr. Celia Banting

Requests for permission to make copies of any part of the work should be mailed to the following address:

Wighita Press
P.O. Box 30399
Little Rock, Arkansas, 72260-0399

www.wighitapress.com

This is a work of fiction. Names of characters, places, and incidents are products of the author's imagination and are used fictitiously and are not to be construed as real. Any resemblance to actual events, locales, organizations, or persons, living or dead, is purely coincidental.

Library of Congress Cataloging-in-Publication Data

Banting, Celia
I Only Said I Had No Choice/Dr. Celia Banting – 1st Edition
p. cm.
ISBN 0-9786648-0-9 (paperback)

1. Therapeutic novel 2. Suicide prevention 3. Anger management
4. Codependence

Library of Congress Control Number: 2006928583

Layout by Michelle VanGeest
Cover production by Luke Johnson

Printed by Dickinson Press, Grand Rapids, Michigan, USA

Issues addressed in this book:

Suicide prevention

Anger management

Behavioral choices and their consequences

Personal responsibility

The biological aspects of feelings

Fight and flight response

The effects of anger upon cognitive processes and communication

The impact of aggressive non-verbal communication upon
the self and others

Relaxation techniques

Adult co-dependence

Coping with abusive stepparents

Two-chair technique to explore empathy

Guided imagery techniques

Symbolism

Coping with blame and injustice

Dedicated to Erica Elsie and Luke.

Acknowledgments

My grateful thanks go to my proofreader and typesetter, Michelle VanGeest, who frees me from my dyslexic brain, and replaces my mother's voice. Thanks to Bev, my stray-word spotter, too. I thank my dear brother, Steve, for his computer expertise, and my wonderful husband, Des, for the inspiration and support he gives me. Thank you to Luke and Sam for their faith, inspiration and talent. Thank you to my dear friend Vicki for her guiding sense of style.

Thank you to all my psychotherapy tutors and colleagues at the Metanoia Institute, London, for teaching me about human nature, psychopathology, growth and recovery.

I thank the good Lord for giving me a lively imagination, and I also thank my parents for moving to the Isle of Wight, "the land that bobs in and out of view, depending upon the sea mist."

Chapter One

"**S**hane, stop it, son," a female guard shouts at me, as two male guards slam me to the floor; my face smarts as the carpet skins a layer off my cheek.

"He ain't gonna stop it; get the nurse to draw up a shot," one of the men growls as he lies across me. "I've got him; get his legs."

I feel my ankles being grabbed and no matter how hard I buck and struggle, I can't move. Moments later my pants are yanked down over my buttocks and a needle fires into me. I want to scream out in pain but I grit my teeth and hiss every cuss word I can think of to let out the agony of being violated and lying spread-eagled on the floor beneath two guards who tell me I'm a worthless piece of rubbish.

I finally lie stock-still and they get off me gingerly, and as they do I leap to my feet and swing at them, my anger ablaze. I hate them; I hate everybody, and most of all, my mom.

I howl as they grab me and wrench my arms backwards, pushing me towards the segregation unit. I don't care anymore; no one can hurt me anymore, even though my arms are dropping off and my ass hurts like hell. I fall in a heap as they throw me through the door and slam it shut, but despite every part of me hurting I leap up and kick at the door, trying to open it as they fumble with the lock.

There's nothing I can do and the powerlessness twists my guts, so I spit at the Perspex window where they're laughing at me and shouting.

"You'll stay in there until you learn to behave yourself. You're not at home now kid, this is juvenile detention and you will follow directions."

I spit again as they leave, laughing.

I hammer on the door and yell every foul word I've ever heard until my throat is hoarse, yet it does no good. I'm stuck in here and they're outside sitting around a table drinking soda and laughing about me, loud enough so that I can hear. My fists are raw from hammering on the door, and my toes hurt where I've been kicking. There's nothing I can do but stop, and as the medication starts to dull my senses, although not the pain in my ass, I fall away from the door and slump to the floor.

There's a camera in the ceiling and I know they're watching me, so I turn onto my side and curl up into a ball so that they can't see my face; I'd rather die than let them see the tears pouring down my face. I'm filled with fear and shame; I can't cry in here, I can't cry anywhere, I don't dare. And yet I can't help it—tears roll down my cheeks, and as my face rests against the cold hard floor, they roll down into my ear and plop onto the floor. I can barely breathe from the sobs that shudder through me as I try desperately to still my body so that the guards won't guess that I'm crying, as they watch me on the camera yards away beyond the locked door.

The medication swamps the desperation that rages through me. My stomach curdles with longing for the mother I detest. The thought of her releases a wave of sobs that wrack their way through my body, and I clamp my hand over my mouth so that no sound escapes from me to seep under the door and let the guards hear my pain. Yet as I try desperately to control myself, my thoughts let me down, and try as I might to rid myself of her, she sits in my head and ravages my heart.

It hasn't always been this way, with me hating her with more venom than is found in a snake-pit, and as the medication creeps through me, tugging at my angst, my anger, my hatred, and wills a calm to come over me, I find that she slips past the fortress I've built to protect myself from her betrayal.

I lie on my back, my tears spent, as her violet eyes bore into my soul, and a part of me that is unaware of the pain in my body longs for her, for the comfort of her arms. Something awful has happened between me and my mom; it never used to be this way; there was only us, no one else. I don't know how to live without my life being the way it was, the only way I had ever known until *he* turned up. It's all *his* fault; none of this would have happened and I wouldn't be in jail if she hadn't married *him*.

I don't remember my dad; he left when I was a baby, telling Mom that he didn't want to be tied down with a screaming brat, and you know, I don't miss him, I don't even care that he left, although I know that Mom cried a lot as I grew up because she was alone. Other kids ask about my dad, kids who have a dad, not kids who don't—we seem to know that it's something we guys just don't talk about. It's more than that for me, though; I *really* don't care. I'm glad he left, because me and my mom spent every minute together, every minute. Some people might think that's weird but I don't care, it was wonderful...I was hers and she was mine and there wasn't anyone else. We didn't need anyone else, well, I didn't, but she obviously did.

A jet of pain and anger flashes through me as her betrayal edges next to thoughts of him. I *hate* him. It surely can't be right to hate someone that much; our pastor tells us hate is bad, so I must be damned for all time because I hate him with every fiber of my being. If it weren't for him my mom and I would still be happy...we didn't need anyone else. Why did she have to go and marry him? Why?

There's a pain in my jaw where my teeth are so tightly clenched together as thoughts of *him* filter through me, even though I don't want them to. I don't want to think of anything, nothing, not *him* and not my mom, and as my tears dry upon my grimy, raw face, while I lie on my back with my muscles soft and slack, oblivion creeps over me.

I'm nestling next to her, her arm firmly around me and she's squealing with fear and delight. I can feel my fists taught around the bar in front of us as the fairground Ferris wheel soars high into the sky, the music churning out beneath us. The lights of the town twinkle in a golden carpet for as far as I can see, and I know that I'm yelling with excitement, while my mom is squealing, her eyes wide. I had jumped up and down until she'd agreed to take me to the fair, and I know that she didn't really want to go, but I did. Everyone at school had been and I just had to go as well, so she let me pull her down the street and across the park. She even gave in when I nagged her to go on the rides with me. The Ferris wheel stopped when we were hanging from the top and it seemed to swing there for ages as more people sat in the seats far beneath us. Mom even stopped squealing as the swinging slowed and she looked out at our town and the lights far below us. As the wheel cranked up and we began our descent she laughed, and the grip of her arm around me made me feel safe, protected, and as if I were a king; as if I were the only thing that mattered to her.

She let me drag her onto every ride and, even though she was pale and giddy, she laughed, and we laughed together. She carried the goldfish swimming lazily around in a plastic bag, and I had a stuffed dog under my arm, and we ate corn-dogs on the way home. I couldn't wait to get to school the next day to tell my friends and my teacher about everything that had happened, about the lights, the smells, the thrill of the rides. The thrill of winning, the thrill of being with my mom and knowing that no one, anywhere, could share in what we had between us.

I can't feel my body and my thoughts are jumbled; I'm completely unable to stop them from cascading in upon me, even though I long for them to stop. The memories of the days when my mom and I were the only thing that mattered in the universe are sweet yet devastating, for to have loved and lost is far more painful than to never have loved at all.

The floor jars my hipbone as my troubled dreams flow through me.

We're lying on the sofa watching the television, my homework done after she'd sat painstakingly helping me to find the right answers and write them neatly in my book. My head nestled into her as she shook, laughing at the images on the television and, although I didn't understand the joke, I laughed too.

My school friends constantly asked me if I missed my dad, so did my school counselor, but how could I possibly miss my dad when I had such a great mom... there was no room for him...there was no room for anyone other than me and my mom.

The cold, hard floor bites into my hip and I'm vaguely aware of turning over. If there was no room for anyone other than me and my mom, how come she invited *him* into our lives?

I'm vaguely aware that a moan escapes my lips, a moan whose origins rest with the pain in my ass from my shot, from the hatred I feel towards *him*, and for the awful emptiness I feel without the mom I used to know. The pain inside me is worse than the pain of the floor jarring against my shot site...it's more than I can stand, so I shut it out as I pull myself to my feet.

My head hurts and it feels woozy, as if it belongs to someone else, and right now I wish it did. I wish that every part of me belonged to someone else, in fact I wish that *I* was someone else. I'd even rather be one of these guys in here that has never had a relationship with their moms, for surely their pain would be less than mine. I mean, if you've never had something, how do you know what you're miss-ing? But for me, I've had it all, I was everything to my mom yet she took it away from me when she met *him*, and so I know the pain of losing what you once had. Right now I wish I'd never had it, never known such love, for to lose it has to be harder than never having had it; well, that's what I think, anyway.

I look through the Perspex window and the guards are still sitting at their table playing cards. One of them notices me and then they all look around.

One walks towards the door with the key in his hand and he shouts through the door, "You gonna hold it together if I open the door?"

I nod, not having the energy to argue with him. He jams his body against the door, while trying to turn the key, then it opens, and I feel a rush of cool air upon my face.

"Go to bed, son," he says kindly, and I stumble past him along the hall to my cell, and as I fall onto my bed, I can hear him locking my door. He looks through the small window and says, "Have a better day tomorrow, okay?" I turn to face the wall, grateful for the relative softness of the mattress on my ass.

All too soon it's morning and my door's being unlocked.

"Get up! Get into the shower and get dressed, now!"

My head and ass hurt like hell but I sit on the side of my bed and take in my surroundings. I've never been to jail before and my stomach's in shreds. I can hear kids calling out, cuss words flying through the air and guards yelling, "Keep it down." I don't know what to do. I don't want to leave my room because I don't know what's waiting for me outside my cell door. There are kids everywhere and the noise is intimidating, but I have no choice because if I've learned anything, it's that if you don't appear to be strong and unafraid you'll get picked on. I can't let that happen, so I grab the towel at my open door and follow the other boys to the shower. There are kids milling everywhere and I try to ignore them as best I can, but it's difficult because they start on me as soon as I walk into the shower with my towel over my shoulder.

"Hey! Fresh meat on the line," a kid shouts and everyone turns to stare at me. My stomach turns to jelly and I need the bathroom urgently. I don't know what to do. My head tells me to front it out and walk past them, make a witty or caustic comment that'll put them in their place, and show them that I'm not afraid. Only I *am* afraid, very afraid, and they can see it in my face, or maybe they can smell it...I don't know. I only know that they know, and they advance towards me.

I stand still, terrified, the contents of my stomach turning to liquid, threatening to roll down my leg if I should move. As they step towards me, their bodies naked and glistening with water droplets, the kid in the front leers at me and I feel sick.

"So, fresh meat, what's for breakfast then?" He holds his penis in his hand and begins to rub it.

The others are edging their way around me. There's a scream inside me that longs to echo around the shower; a scream that is mingled with terror at the threatening crowd before me and the anger towards my mom, for if it weren't for her marrying *him*, I'd never be in this place.

I try desperately to remember the Tae Kwon Do I learned as a kid and snap into a defensive pose, praying that my bluff will make them back off, but although they falter for a second, they laugh and then begin to edge toward me. Terror rages through me and at this moment I'm prepared to kill. No one is going to violate me. Last night, when I got a shot, will be the last time that I'll let anyone hurt me or leave me powerless.

I can feel the muscles in my arms tense and I remember everything my teachers taught me about frightening an aggressor off by making lots of noise, so I roar. My fear is beyond my control and it sits in my clenched teeth, ready to bite anyone or anything that comes anywhere near me.

My fists are so tight that I can feel my nails biting into the palms of my hands as I brace myself for the fight of my life, but it doesn't happen.

"Stop! Right now! Stop! Get out of the shower now, and get dressed. You're to be in the cafeteria in five minutes."

The voice comes from a huge black man, bald, muscular and formidable, yet there's something in his face that reassures me, slightly, just slightly, for I don't know if I'll ever trust anyone again in my life, ever. Yet suddenly all the kids have disappeared to their own cells to get dressed. I'm so grateful to him for saving me that I long to throw my arms around him and thank him over and over again, but I don't. I just follow his directions and hope that the compliance I'm showing lets him know that I'm more grateful than he'll ever know.

There's no mirror in my cell; I guess they think I'll cut myself with it, so we're not allowed one. I don't care though, my hair's short and I just run my fingers through it and throw my clothes on. I stand in my cell doorway ready to go to the cafeteria. I don't feel hungry, in fact I feel really sick. Several boys flip me off when the guard isn't watching and others flash gang signs at me, signs that let me know they're gonna get me when they get the opportunity. I pray that they can't see the fear I feel deep inside of me. I grit my teeth and try to set my face in an aggressive, dangerous pose, one that tells them I'm not frightened of them, even though I'm terrified. I can't let them see that I'm scared or they'll have me.

Is it this hard being a girl? It seems that for boys you have to be tough or else the other kids will rip you to pieces, and sometimes even the toughest kids get ripped to pieces. Do girls have to go through this? Do they?

"Move on, and no talking," the guard shouts, and we shuffle in a line along the hall to the cafeteria.

A miserable looking man with dirty fingernails slops some scrambled eggs onto a paper plate and gives me a plastic spoon. I feel sick, but not as sick as I feel when I sit down and a kid walks behind me and spits over my shoulder. A glob of spittle lands on the clumps of yellow powered egg. Even though I feel nauseated and scared I dart out of my seat and jump on the kid's back, punching him in the head. I have to because everyone's watching to see what I'll do.

He shoots around and slams his fist into my face; pain numbs my senses, and tears spring into my eyes. I'm horrified that my eyes are leaking, and so an anger borne out of fear of ridicule courses through my body like a trapped wild animal, and ignoring the agony in my face, and the salty blood in my mouth, I hammer my fists into his body.

I'm roaring but I can hardly hear myself as all the kids are on their feet, yelling, and I'm barely aware of the guards plowing through the kids to separate us. I only really notice when two of them slam me to the cafeteria floor and my head collides with the stone-cold tiles, and when the pain in my shoulders hits me as my arms are wrenched behind my back.

They yank me up and haul me out of the cafeteria kicking and screaming. Although I'm in agony I'm not going to let any of them know; all they'll see of me is my anger. My anger is my truth and my anger is my protector.

They throw me into my cell and lock the door. I'm on twenty-four hour lockdown and they say that if I don't shape up I'll be on another twenty-four hour lockdown tomorrow. Can't they see that's what I want? I'm safe in my cell, safe from all the kids that are like animals in a place where the survival of the fittest rules. I'll do whatever I have to in order to be separated from them, and if that means acting out, then that's what I'll do.

The only problem with being on lockdown is that there's nothing to do and too much time to think. At least last night when I was given a shot the medication deadened my senses and it was hard to think, but right now all I have is me, four walls and my thoughts.

I curse my brain, I don't want to think. Thinking is dangerous—it takes me to a place where I can't be sure that I can control myself. Something insidious happens when I think, as if my thoughts are connected to tentacles, like octopus tentacles, that search and creep, seeking to connect with my feelings. I don't want to feel...I never want to feel again, it's too painful, and yet my thoughts seek my feelings and pounce upon them..

I punch the cold stark wall and barely wince as blood trickles from my knuckles. The pain is a distraction, one that hopefully will sever the connection between my thoughts and my feelings...I'll do anything to stop myself from feeling. If I go crazy maybe they'll give me another shot, and then I won't have to think or feel anything. Yes, that's what I'll do, because I can't stand the pain inside me.

I start screaming and smashing my head on the door; they'll have to come and stop me soon. My mouth is filthy and I cuss every foul word I know and hammer on the door with my fists, even when I fear that I'll pass out with the pain.

I don't have to wait long before I hear the key turn in the lock and two huge men armed with a mattress in front of them slam into me, knocking me clean across the room. I'm pinned against the opposite wall with the mattress threatening to suffocate me. There's nowhere for me to flail my arms and legs and the frustration soars within me so that when they pull the mattress off me I lash out at them, but it's no good. They're ready for me, and again I'm smashed down on the floor, but this time it's a welcomed relief when the needle slams into my buttock.

I pray they've given me enough to make the pain in my face, and the pain in my heart, go away.

I'm instantly still and silent, having got what I wanted...oblivion.

"He's drug seeking," a guard says. "Don't give him anymore, you'll turn him into an addict."

I want to tell him to shut up but the drugs are speeding through my body and my mouth won't work.

"You're right," another guard says. He lowers his face so that he's down on my level and hisses into my face, "Well, next time you pull a stunt like this, hurting yourself, you'll be strapped to a wooden bed. They'll be no more medication, no more drugs. Do you hear me?"

But I barely hear him as the medication slices all the sharp edges off my consciousness.

It's ages later when I wake up. I know that because the sun casts shadows in my cell and they're long and dim. I wish that I hadn't woken up because the pain in my face is excruciating; not only is there a carpet burn on my cheek from last night but my face feels like jelly where that creep pummeled his fists into me. Not to mention the pain in my forehead where I smashed my head onto the cell door to get attention.

I can't help it, a tear rolls down my burning cheek. I don't dare brush it away for fear it'll hurt too much, so I just let it slide down my face and pool in my ear. I'm only fourteen; how can I be in such a place? I've never been in trouble before, ever. I don't understand how things can change so quickly and so dramatically. Am I supposed to know these things when I'm just fourteen? I'm supposed to be old enough to cope with changes in my life that I didn't ask for, supposed to be grown up and accept a new man into my life and call him "Dad."

Damn my thoughts...I don't want to think about

him, or Mom, but they flow over me like a tide racing over a seashore.

It's always been just Mom and me, always, and we've never needed anybody else, well, that's what I thought. A wave of sickness flows through me as I realize that I'm wrong and that my mom didn't care as much about me as I cared about her. I feel betrayed. I'll never love again, not anyone. How can you recover from betrayal by your mother? And yet just thinking about her hurts so badly that I long for her, for the cozy, fun times we had...times that were snuffed out the moment *he* walked through the door.

I don't understand it. Why did she even want to find a man? I heard her over and over saying that after my dad left she'd never go with another man, so why did she change her mind? Wasn't what we had enough? I thought it was.

I've listened to my friends at school say terrible things about their moms and it shocked me because I thought that everyone had a relationship like I had with my mom; we played, we talked, we hugged and watched TV together on the sofa after stuffing as much pizza into our mouths as we could possibly manage. Didn't every kid have that kind of relationship with their moms? I learned that they didn't, and part of me felt lucky, but a part of me felt sad for them. I felt like I had a relationship with my mom that I couldn't share; it was too precious to me, yet sometimes I felt a bit embarrassed because I thought it could be misunderstood by others who obviously didn't know how wonderful such a relationship could be.

At times I felt alone because I couldn't talk to anyone about my relationship with my mom, as no one I know has ever described the same spark with their moms that I feel with mine – well, felt. I don't feel it anymore, and that's what I mean about it being easier to have never loved before; then you don't know what you're missing. I certainly know what I'm missing, and I wish I didn't.

A key turning in the lock jolts me from my thoughts and I'm glad; I don't want to think about anything.

"Get up, now!"

I don't know what to do, whether to be belligerent and lie here just to piss him off, or whether to stop this act and do what he says so that I don't have to pretend anymore. He makes up my mind for me by walking over to my hard, unrelentless bed, and pulling at my arm.

"I said, get up!"

Immediately the bile in my throat rises, and I yank my arm away from him.

"Oh, so we've still got an attitude, have we? Well, that's easy to deal with. You can stay in here for the rest of the night. Whatever," and he walks away. Moments later the door opens again, only I can't be bothered to get off my bed to put up a fight, and a tray of cold food is slid across the floor, landing with a bump against my bed. I'm not eating that, it's disgusting. Despite the biting hunger in my belly I resist, damn them, damn my mom, and most of all, damn *him*; I will not succumb. Resistance is the only power I have right now; they've taken everything away from me, and while I'm in my cell, safe from the animals outside who want blood from the "fresh meat on the line," I can vent my anger safely. I don't care, and as the tension flows through me, I turn on to my side, my fists clenched, my teeth jammed together and my knees locked under my chin, and I face the wall. I wish that my mind and heart were as bare as the wall before me.

I've no idea how long I lie facing the wall, my body tense, my hatred acute and raw, and my stomach knotted with hunger, before I finally fall asleep.

Chapter Two

I wake early, the pain in my body robbing me of sleep, and I lie still, dull and miserable. I don't know what to do. The shadows are creeping across the floor of my cell, and I know that soon the door will be unlocked and I'll have to face going into the shower again. I can't do it, I just can't. I know the others are gonna get me—they won't let it rest—so as I lie here I work out what to do. If I go into the shower and they start on me, I'll have to fight again, but there are too many of them. I may not be so lucky today to be saved by the guard.

I can feel the sweat pouring off me although the cell is cold and my heart is hammering in my chest. I know that I can't allow myself to get to the shower; I'll have to act out before then.

I hear a key in the door. An echoing sound comes from a prison cell door when it's being opened that's quite unlike any other door; it lets me know that there's a space in the thickness of the door, which also tells me that it's reinforced and that escape is impossible. But I don't want to escape from this cell because, even though it's designed to alienate me from everyone else, that's exactly what I want, so that I'll be safe.

All too soon the guards open the door and I suddenly feel sick. It's now or never, so as the door opens I charge at the guard and pummel my fists into any part of his body that I can, which isn't much since another guard runs over and grabs me.

The kids are all hooting and hollering but I'm not safe yet. If I calm down too soon they'll send me off to the showers, so I kick out at the guards who grip me firmly as I try to claw at them; I even try to bite them. It works and they march me down the hall, but I don't go quietly because I don't want them to think that this is what I wanted, so I buck and struggle.

"I told you yesterday that if you act out like this again you won't be getting anymore shots...you're drug seeking. You're not getting any more," a guard shouts at me over my cussing.

I call him something really bad as they throw me into a cell that stinks of pee and lock the door quickly. Although I've got what I wanted, I'm so fired up that I can't calm down, and I'm not pretending when I smash myself against the door over and over, welcoming the pain, which is nothing compared to the pain inside me.

I don't stop. I can't stop. It feels like something has set loose inside me and everything I've felt over the past two years roars out of me, and although the screaming sounds far away, I'm vaguely aware that it's coming from me. It's as if I'm floating above myself, watching a crazy person, one that looks like me but isn't me.

Suddenly the door is yanked open and it all happens so fast. I'm still screaming, my arms and legs splaying everywhere, but then I'm lifted up as if I'm completely weightless and slammed onto the heavy wooden bed in the corner of the room.

A guard shouts over my screaming but I barely hear him.

"I told you, didn't I, you're not getting a shot."

He looks like he hates me, but not as much as I hate him right this minute and I spit right into his face, feeling a flash of triumph as he looks stunned.

There are hands weighing heavily all over my body and I can't move, as I'm spread-eagled on the hard wooden bed that has no mattress. I can't do anything but spit and smash my head over and over against the bed.

"You can stop that too," a guard says, "I've got something for that," and he stops me by placing a pillow under my head and I can't do anything about it as the leather cuffs around my ankles and wrists hold me tight.

They walk away ignoring my foul mouth. My

throat is raw from screaming and every part of me is tingling with the rage that burns through me. I don't know how to stop it from consuming me and as I continue to scream and thrash my head about, nudging the pillow out from under me so that I can smash my head against the bed again, a small voice inside me tells me I've lost it and there's no way back from this.

Somehow through my raging I feel something; my arms and legs are restrained by leather cuffs but I'm struggling and bucking so much that I can feel the chaffing of the leather on my wrists. My screaming slows to sobs as I catch my breath and I focus upon the leather against my wrist, which starts to smart but the pain is more a sensation and nothing compared to the pain I've endured during the past two years. I rub and rub my wrist knowing that it's biting into me; yes, that's good, deeper, harder, faster. I want out of here. If I have to feel pain, I want the hurt I feel to be on the surface, not the hurt inside, which is unbearable.

It feels wet and the rubbing gets easier.

"Get the nurse," I hear a guard shout and so I rub my wrist against the leather furiously before they come to stop me, and as they do so I start screaming again. As the needle stabs into my thigh the nurse's lips twist into a vicious hiss.

"So you want to be a drug addict, do you? See if I care."

But I don't want any more shots, I don't want to calm down, I don't want the woozy feeling it forces upon you, robbing you of your reason, I just want to be dead, to make this all go away. I want to be as dead as my heart feels right now.

They walk away leaving me strapped to the hard bed, and although my body suddenly feels heavy, and my head hasn't enough energy to nudge the pillow back out from beneath it so that I can carry on hurting myself, I can still move my wrist.

I lie there struggling to keep the last fragment of my mind focused upon what I have to do, and it's all I can do to manage it, but despite my body being loaded with drugs that rob me of my mind and movement, I force my hand to keep moving. I have to die; there's no way out. I can't stay in juvenile detention with these creeps, and I can't go home to be around my mom who's chosen *him* over me.

I can't bear to think of her so I try desperately to channel my flagging energy into gouging at the open wound on my wrist. I can't feel any pain except that in my heart and I long for it to be over—so I rub and I rub until the drugs take me down.

• • • •

I don't know what day it is; every part of me is in agony. I try to raise my arm because my wrist hurts badly and then I remember what I was doing. How come I'm not dead? Damn the drugs, I must have passed out before I finished gouging the hole in my wrist.

I'm lying on a bed and it's moving; there's a guy sitting next to me, and he turns when he sees me moving.

"Hi, how're you doing?"

I don't speak. I wonder if I am dead after all. This guy's too nice. Perhaps he's a being in the afterlife; he certainly can't be a human being. I try desperately to gather my thoughts that don't seem to want to belong to me, as I keep drifting off into unconsciousness.

The next time I wake up I realize that I'm in an ambulance, and with that realization comes the fact that I'm still alive, and that means that the pain of my mom choosing some creep over me and not wanting me is still real. I try so hard to be strong but the drugs flowing through my body betray me and tears flow down my face. I'm vaguely aware of the chaffing around my neck where the orange prison jump-suit rubs me, and as I try to move I can hear the clanking of chains; I'm shackled. How can I be shackled? I'm only fourteen. A year ago I was in the bell choir at church and was on the football and basketball teams.

The tears seem to have a life of their own and refuse to obey me. They roll down my face and suddenly my nose is stopped up and I can barely breathe.

"Here, have a tissue," the guy sitting next to me

says, and I try to blow my nose but the chains clank when I move my arms, and pull on my ankles that are attached to them.

"You look like a good kid. What's going on?"

His kindness knocks the wind out of me, like I've been kicked in the stomach, and any resolve I have leaves me, and I sob like a baby. I'm embarrassed, humiliated, but he just hands me another tissue. "It'll work out, really, it will if you want it to. They'll help you at Beach Haven, you'll be all right."

"Where?"

"Beach Haven is a place where kids go to get help with their problems; I've taken loads of kids there since becoming a paramedic. It's a good place."

"Why am I going there? I've got to go to court because I threatened to kill my stepfather."

"The judge has ordered that you go to Beach Haven to work on your problems rather than be sent to juvenile. Make the most of it, kid, the staff there will do everything they can to help you."

"I don't want help, I just want to die," I say, wondering who I'll have to fight in this new place.

"Listen, my son was about your age when he died of cancer. Don't wish your life away and certainly not in front of me or I might have to blacken your other eye."

He punches me gently on the arm and I'm ashamed of myself. I mutter, "Sorry."

"You're pretty lucky to be allowed to go there

because it's a special place, not like all the other facilities around for kids. This one is for kids without behavioral or anger problems, and by the state of your face, I would guess that you have problems with both."

"Not usually," I say, pouting. He doesn't know me. Just because my face is black and blue and I look like a thug doesn't mean that I am one. I feel the urge to stick up for my reputation by telling him that I was in the bell choir two years ago, but I don't want him to see how far I've fallen.

"What're you usually like then?" he asks, but I don't want to tell him because that'll mean talking about my mom and *him*, so I just lie there as the ambulance passes a train that blasts its horn.

He tries to make me talk and I want to tell him to "shut up" but somewhere deep inside me I'm grateful that he doesn't give up on me.

"Beach Haven is such a cool place...I wish they had places for adults because I'd book myself in, that's for sure. It's like being in a comfortable time out, right by the beach, it's so peaceful. Mind you, it's not a place where you can slide by and do nothing—you have to work on your problems and be really truthful. It's not for everyone. Your probation officer must have thought you could make it. I'm glad for you. Oh, look, we're here. Work hard, okay, kid? This is your opportunity to make it. Y'know, life is precious. I know it's hard for you at the moment, and I don't know anything about your problems. All I know is that it's hard to be a teenager, always has been, but work hard, okay? Don't wish to be dead, life can be good, and if you can't see that at the moment then consider that some kids your age don't get a choice as to whether they live or not; live life for them if you can't live life for yourself at the moment."

I feel so bad and I don't know what to say. I still want to die but I can't say it anymore because his son is dead.

"I'm sorry, kid. I miss my boy. I didn't mean to lay all that on you; it's just that life *is* so precious no matter what's happening to you now. You can make it. Don't give up."

Suddenly I'm being lowered onto the ground and they're wheeling me through the entrance doors. I'm scared but nowhere near as scared as I was after the police arrested me at school for threatening to kill my stepfather. I hadn't even made the threat to him; I'd just said it to my friend but a teacher heard me. It was just something kids say. I wouldn't have killed him, or anyone, although I'd give anything to make him go away so that my mom and I could be together like it was before.

I don't want to think about her because it's too painful, so I push the thoughts away and look around.

I'm in a large reception area with two staircases,

one to the right and one to the left of me. The paramedics say, "Hi" to a lady in reception, who smiles at me. Above her is a sign that says, "Welcome, remember what peace there may be found in silence, rest here and grow." They turn left and I try to take in all the images that flash past me as they walk along the corridor. There are pictures on the wall, the sort that I draw when I'm angry or hurt, pictures that show what's happening inside.

I look up at the ceiling as they push me along and there are even pictures pinned up there, ones that say, "Each person has a story to tell," and "Grow if you dare to." There are wild paintings that tell me the kids who painted them felt the same way I'm feeling right now, and somehow I feel a sense of calm come over me. I don't know what it is and I have no words for it, but I sense that this is a place where I won't have to behave like an animal in order to keep myself safe. I'm scared and apprehensive, but the rage and terror that drove me to behave like a wild animal seem to have left me. I'm relieved, for I hate who I've become; it isn't the real me.

"Hi, my name is Miss Tina," a lady says, smiling at me. "Welcome to Beach Haven. Just be yourself and you'll end up growing into yourself. This is a safe place for kids, kids that want to grow. We won't let anything hurt you while you're here, and we'll show you how to stop things hurting you when you leave. Are you hungry?"

Suddenly I'm ravenous, so I nod.

"We saved you some pizza. I've never known a kid that doesn't like pizza," she laughs with the paramedic. "We saved you some, too."

"Oh, good. See I told you, Shane, this is a good place."

He helps me stand up, and the guard that had traveled with the driver, the big black guy who saved me in the shower, steps forward with the key to the shackles that are supposed to keep my arms and legs from going crazy and from escaping. Don't they know that I don't want to escape? For suddenly this place feels like the warmest, safest place that I've ever been in and escape seems awful, just awful.

The guard unlocks my hands and I wince as the pain in my wrists smarts badly. Then he bobs down to pull the chains from my ankles, and as he does he gives me a gift; he lets me know that he trusts me. He's seen me fight like a wild animal in juvenile and he knows that I could hurt him while he's kneeling down, but as soon as he slips the key into the lock he looks up at me—trust is there in his gaze. There's no way that I can let him down even if I wanted to, but I don't want to. I feel small and humble that he should give me the opportunity to prove myself to him for he saved me, and I want him to think well of me even though he knows how badly I behaved in juvenile.

"Have you got anything he can wear?" he asks.

Miss Tina brings me some pajamas with rabbits on them and just as I'm about to say, "I can't wear them," I see both the paramedics and the guard shoot me a look that says, "Don't you dare," so I mutter "Thanks," and disappear into the bathroom to change from my prison suit. I'd rather wear rabbits than the orange jump suit that tells everyone you're a piece of rubbish. I kick off my orange slip-on plastic shoes and go barefooted, stretching my feet and relishing in their and my freedom. The rabbit pajamas feel cozy and warm and suddenly I'm starving; it's ages since I ate.

It's a bizarre moment with Miss Tina, the guard and two paramedics sitting around the table eating pizza, with me in my rabbit pajamas, my throat still raw from all my screaming, and my face as raw as fresh hamburger meat.

We eat until it's all gone and suddenly they're gone too. A flash of panic courses through me, not because I'm scared; I'm apprehensive because I don't know where I'm going to sleep, and I don't know if I'm going to have to fight anyone to keep myself safe. My stomach's churning as well because I don't know if I've got the guts to be totally honest to "tell my story, or to grow, if I dare." It all sounds frightening.

I don't know what to say now that it's just Miss Tina and me, and suddenly my tongue doesn't work. She goes to a cupboard and puts a tin on the table with a rabbit on the lid.

"Help yourself to cookies," she says, grinning at me. "As nice as you look in rabbit pajamas, we need to get your mom to bring your clothes tomorrow."

Suddenly the bite of cookie in my mouth tastes like cardboard.

"I don't want her here, I don't ever want to see her again," I snap, putting the cookie down.

"What's going on? Why do you feel that way about your mom? I spoke to her earlier and she doesn't feel that way about you."

I'm instantly angry and lean forward. "I don't want to have anything to do with her, that's all," and I know I must look stupid being so angry, dressed in rabbit pajamas, with my face all red.

She doesn't move, nor does she react to my anger, and I don't know what to do. I just stand there feeling hateful and stupid at the same time. I can't stomp off to my room because I don't know where it is yet, nor can I run away because I don't know where I am, and more importantly I'm dressed in stupid rabbit pajamas.

She speaks very calmly. "Shane, here we face our problems and our feelings even though they may be painful. We don't tolerate aggression. This place is a safe place, a safe haven, where you'll never be judged and you'll be accepted for who you are, but those that stay here are committed to facing their problems rather than acting out to avoid facing them. We are truthful here; there are no lies and no rescues. I know what happened in juvenile and you need to know that such behavior won't be tolerated here."

My anger is still flaring. I feel that she's scolding me, yet her voice is so soft and calm that it doesn't fit with all the scoldings I've had in the past. Then it dawns on me that perhaps she isn't scolding me and so I've got no reason to be angry or defensive, so I edge back into my seat and hang my head. Okay, so I'm allowed to pout a little.

"We'll help you while you're here to explore the reasons for your anger and to find a safer way to express your feelings."

I want to say something ugly to let her know that I already know the reasons for my anger and aggression. I'm angry because my mom betrayed me, and I was aggressive because I was completely terrified that I was going to be gang-raped in the shower at juvenile. I already know. I can feel my anger rising again, but my bottom lip sinks lower as I say nothing.

"It's not that anger is a forbidden feeling, it's not; anger can be healthy when it's not masking your true feelings."

I pick up my half-eaten cookie and take a bite so that I don't have to answer her.

"Often people substitute one feeling for another. Often people are angry or aggressive when really they're sad or scared."

I wish I hadn't taken another bite because her words make a lump come into my throat and I can barely swallow. She's just described how I feel and she knows that my anger isn't really me, not the real me.

"One of the reasons why we don't take kids here who act out is because it disrupts everyone else. Suddenly the kids who really want to work on their problems, and who are brave enough to do so, feel that the environment isn't safe anymore. They can't be sure that they will be taken care of when they reveal their most painful thoughts and feelings if some kid is taking all the attention by acting out, so they stop sharing and they become fearful. Oh, they may not show it but deep inside that's how it is for them. Most of the kids here know all about anger and aggression, and when faced with it again they clam up and they're too scared to share their innermost thoughts and feelings around people who act out. I understand them; I would be too. Besides that, aggression is a cop out."

"What d'you mean?"

"Acting out is an easy way of avoiding your feelings. Say someone challenges you about something and you don't want to answer. What better way to avoid answering than to kick off and act out? Suddenly all the energy in the room is focused upon containing you so that you don't hurt anyone or yourself, and in doing so the focus is sucked away from those who want to work on their problems. The kid who acts out gets all the attention without having done anything to work on his problems; it's a cop out, one that's very damaging to all the other kids."

I chew and swallow.

"So why'd you let me come here then?"

"That's a good question. I always take a history from the parents when kids are referred here; it helps me understand what's going on at home."

I'm confused, for if she's spoken to my mom, then why am I here? My mom is bound to tell her that I've been hateful and have done anything and everything to get rid of *him*, even threatening at school to kill him; so why am I here?

She smiles at me before answering and suddenly some of my anger—or is it fear—slips away from me.

"Your mom told me that you used to be in the bell choir and I figured that any kid who enjoyed making music and was committed to practicing must have had something happen to him to make him become so aggressive. Being creative and violent just don't go together in my book."

I'm beginning to feel like a bug under a microscope, for again she's just described how it is for me.

I'm silent, my cookie eaten, but because I don't want to say anything, I pick another one out of the tin and start munching.

"To answer your question, Shane, you were accepted here because most people in your life see your current behavior as being out of character, and if you should continue along this path you'll mess up a life that was full of promise. We'll do anything we can to prevent that from happening but you have to help us. We can't do anything unless you are willing to help, too."

I take another cookie and say nothing.

"Well, I guess you've got enough to think about, so if you've finished with the cookies I'll show you your room, and tomorrow we'll get your mom to bring in some clothes for you."

I open my mouth to object but she silences me.

"You don't have to see her, but she will be coming, okay?"

I follow her down the hall cleaning my teeth of cookie gunk with my tongue. She leads me up one of the huge staircases and along a corridor in which more pictures drawn by kids hang on the wall.

"This is your room, Shane. It's a beautiful room; you can lie on your bed and listen to the waves roll up the beach. It's so peaceful. Remember, this place is a comfortable time out, a place to rest and grow."

So I lie in my bed feeling cozy in my crazy, soft, rabbit pajamas wondering how things can change so much in just one day. This time last night I was wondering how I was going to avoid gang rape in the shower at juvenile, and here I am, safe, wearing rabbit pajamas. If I wasn't sure that I was awake, and I know I am because my body hurts so much, I'd think that I was lost in some strange surreal dream where rabbits, fists, blood and pain all live miserably together. Yet as I lie here in this warm, clean bed, the pain in my body reminding me that this *is* real, I can hear the waves crashing upon the shore and rushing up the sand, just yards away. I've never heard such a thing and Miss Tina's right...it is peaceful.

Hearing the ocean reminds me that life is going on out there whether I'm in it or not, and whether I feel as if my whole life is falling apart or not. The waves remind me that there are other things that are constant, things that don't change. I like that; it slows my breath and makes me feel calmer.

I suddenly feel a sense of hope; I can't wait for the morning so that I can look out of the window and see the ocean crash upon the shore. My eyes become moist and although I immediately start to get angry with myself, I stop, because there's no one in this room but me, and I don't have to pretend to be strong. A tear seeps out of my eye, despite my fist being clenched, and there's a voice in my head which belongs to *him* that tells me I'm a baby and a mommy's boy, and yet I don't wipe it away. I let it roll and it slips down the side of my face, getting colder as it reaches my ear, then it stops, waiting for the next one to join it, and it comes, followed by another and then another.

I can't stop it from happening and I'm so glad

that Miss Tina gave me a room of my own or else I just know that I'd be fighting by now in an attempt to hide my feelings. But now that I'm alone my feelings are out there, and raw.

As the sobbing wracks my body, the part of me that floats high above and watches tells me to be quiet, someone will hear and then I'll have to fight to save my reputation. I can't be seen to have any feelings, I'm a guy...only girls cry, and then only stupid ones. I bite my pillow, and when that doesn't work I slam my hand over my mouth, ignoring the pain as I knock clumsily into my gouged wrist with my chin. Something bad is happening to me and I can't stop it; everything I've felt over the past two years seems to be flowing out of me in a tidal wave of despair. As I slam the pillow over my face to drown out any escaping sobs, I pray that I stop breathing to make the pain go away, but even that doesn't happen, for something stops me.

Suddenly I'm aware that someone's in the room and I'm filled with shame. How awful to be caught crying dressed in rabbit pajamas! Yet there's not enough time for me to become defensive and get ready to fight, for Miss Tina sits on the edge of my bed. I can see a man standing in the doorway watching, silently, but I ignore him as she puts her arms around me and holds my head towards her.

"Shhh," she says, but I can't. Something's going on inside me that I don't understand; I feel as if I've fallen apart on the outside and on the inside, and as if the only thing that's holding me together is this lady that I don't even know.

Chapter Three

I don't remember falling asleep; all I remember is waking in the night with a start, drenched in sweat and my wrists in agony. My ankles hurt like hell, too, and I realize that my bucking and writhing against the leather restraints didn't just rub my wrists; they rubbed my ankles raw as well. Yet I can't feel sorry for myself as I lie in this bed listening to the rhythmic waves rolling up the shore right outside my window because yesterday, although I wasn't in so much physical pain as I am now, I was in fear of being raped and being beaten up. As I lie here hurting, I can't believe that the terror I felt yesterday has gone and the only thing I feel is the pain in my body and anxiety as to what I will face tomorrow in this place. I can't believe just how much life can change in one day. As the waves blend into the sound of the ceiling fans going round and round,

I pray a silent prayer to a God who I'm not sure is there, but I pray anyway.

I awake to the sounds outside my door; someone's yelling for us to get up...this feels like an unlocked prison, someone is ordering us about. I can't help it, immediately I'm pissed. I've spent the last couple of years being pushed about by *him* and then by juvenile, I'm not going to be pushed around here.

"Time to get up, kid," a man says, so I ignore him. I turn over and pull the covers over my head; my eyes are wide awake, wondering what's going to happen. It's a no man's land, I don't know what to do and I don't know what will happen if I don't get up straight away. I wait under the covers, feeling just a little bit stupid, but then he comes back again and tells me to get up, it's time for breakfast.

I don't move but my ears are acute, listening for signs of him walking towards me, which he does, so I get ready.

"C'mon kid, get up, it's almost time for breakfast."

I have a choice and I don't know what to do. I can swing around and fly at him like I did towards the guards in juvenile, or I can pull the covers tighter around me and ignore him...both will piss him off and let him know that I'm not going to be pushed around.

He comes over to my bed and yanks the covers off while I'm still thinking about what to do.

"C'mon kid, get up, it's nearly time for breakfast."

I jump up, my fists ready, but he stops me by laughing. He almost falls over he's laughing so much.

I don't know what to do; my fists are clenched
yet, how can you punch someone who's rolling about
laughing?

"Hey man, quit," he says, between being bent
double laughing.

I seriously don't know what to do so I just stand
there, and then I realize.

"Cool pajamas," he guffaws, and I don't know
whether to rush at him or run into the bathroom, so
I do neither and just stand there, feeling angry.

"I'm sorry, man, but you just look so funny. Y'know
it's hard to be angry or tough when you're wearing
bunnies."

We stand there looking at each other, him trying
desperately to stifle his laughter and me trying to
work out what to do, whether to be affronted and
fight him or whether to laugh with him. I remember
what Miss Tina said last night about not tolerating
aggression so I unclench my fists. It *is* pretty funny
and I know that if I were in his shoes, I'd laugh like a
stopped up drain, so I grin.

He walks towards me and holds out his hand.

"My name's Ken. You're Shane, aren't you?"

I nod and shake his hand. I feel a sense of relief
and respect for him because he enables me to scram-

ble back from the point where I was about to punch him to a point where I feel like his equal. I don't know how he does it, but he does.

"Here, let me go and see what clothes we've got in the store until your mom brings your own clothes. We can't have you going to the dining room like that, you'll cause a riot."

He turns around chuckling to himself as he leaves, so I go into the bathroom and take a shower. It's heaven standing beneath the steaming jets of water washing all the grime off me, grime that isn't just dirt but foul memories of the gang in the shower at juvenile. I turn off the cold and the water gets hotter and hotter until I wince, but it's still wonderful even though it's beginning to hurt. I want to feel clean, *really* clean, and a little pain is worth it to feel that way.

The mirror is all steamed up so I can't see my bruised and skinned face, although I can still feel it; it hurts like hell. I rub the towel over my body hard even though that hurts too, and I finally feel clean. I gingerly open the door with a towel tied around my waist. Ken has put some sweats by the bathroom door so I snatch them up and pull them on, which isn't easy as the bathroom is so steamy that I'm soaked again in sweat. I rub the towel over the mirror and am shocked at the state of my face; it's swollen and stiff, black and blue. I'm a mess, but I grin at my reflection because everyone that meets me is going to think that I'm hard, and that's not an image that I've ever had, but one that I quite like.

It's not easy being a kid, a boy, especially one that was so close to his mom that people thought it was odd. Then it wasn't easy being so into music and being in the bell choir with all the girls. I loved the music we made; it made me feel excited, although I couldn't tell anyone. The guys at school picked on me about it until I joined the football team and then they left me alone, seeing me as one of them, I guess. When you're a kid it matters a whole lot what others think of you and if they think you're a jerk, your life'll be hell. You have to appear tough—that's the only language they know—and the toughest kids are the ones whose faces show that they've been fighting. Well, that's how it seems to me.

I wipe the mirror again and peer at my battered face; yes, everyone will think I'm tough all right, well, so long as they don't look into my eyes, that is. My eyes hold something unfathomable to me, something I don't want to acknowledge...so I look away and leave the bathroom.

"Hey," a girl says as she passes my door, "How'ya doin'? I'm Alison."

"I'm Shane," I say, embarrassed to be wearing sweats and not my own clothes; but I guess I'm grateful that I'm not still wearing the rabbit pajamas. I shudder at the thought. Can you imagine meeting a girl looking that way?

"What happened to you?" she asks, looking disap-
provingly.

I don't know what to say. I thought she'd see me
as cool, or tough, with my face all beat up, but her
expressions tell me I'm wrong.

"Um, I, um, fell. Yes, I fell down the stairs."

"Yeah, really."

She walks off leaving me embarrassed and with
my heart thumping.

Kids are walking up and down the hall and I feel
like a spare nut in a dismantled car as I stand in my
doorway not knowing what to do. I'm expecting to be
ordered to stand in line and to be silent but it doesn't
happen. Ken just shouts out, "Come on then, let's go
eat," and we all move off in a jumbled group, kids
chatting and laughing running down the stairs.

I feel disorientated; I'd expected to be ordered,
to be pushed about by someone in authority. It's my
experience that adults like being in charge, they like
pushing kids around. Not my mom, of course. Damn,
why did she have to pop into my head...?

I force the thoughts of her away as I walk along
the hall with all the other kids my age. Hey, there
are some hot babes here, cool. Suddenly I wish my
face weren't so battered and bruised because I don't
want them to think I'm a jerk.

It's so hard to be a guy...I'm a jerk if I'm in the
bell choir making music, then I'm a jerk if I fight and
look like a beaten boxer with no brains.

My appetite is raw but with all the thoughts racing through me it leaves and then returns again. I don't know if I'm hungry or if I'm just empty; I'm a bit of both, I think.

I follow everyone, not knowing where I'm going and my stomach begins to rumble...I can smell bacon and sausage patties. There's a big lady with a big smile in the dining room who's putting trays of food on a large table and all the kids are helping themselves to what they want. "Help yourself," she says to me. "Have as much or as little as you want."

I'm reminded of the dirty, miserable man in juvenile who slopped scrambled egg on my tray and I can't believe how different this place is. Suddenly I'm ravenous. I smile at her even though it makes my face smart and she says, "You'll be okay here, kid, we feed you good."

I like her and she cooks better than my mom. I go back for seconds and can't believe that I'm allowed to. I'm stuffing food into my mouth while the others are talking and I pray that no one is watching me and thinks I'm greedy...but right this minute I am. I'm hungry and I'm empty.

No one notices me though, they're all talking, and it dawns on me how different this is. In juvenile we're not allowed to speak; we have to go everywhere in silence, but here everyone is talking as if they're adults in a restaurant...perhaps that's what the staff want us to be...adults. I don't know what to think.

When I finish and I'm so stuffed that I can't move, I sit back and watch everyone. No one bothers with me and I feel a bit left out and awkward. Are they like this with all new kids? They're not very friendly if they are. Then it dawns on me what Miss Tina said last night about violence and aggression making other kids scared, and my face sure as hell speaks of violence. Are they shunning me because my face tells them that I'm violent and aggressive? I hope not. Hell, I was in the bell choir. Violence has been forced upon me by my stepfather and by trying to survive in juvenile. There are some mean kids there, and as I think about it I wonder if they're as mean as they are because they're scared like me and want to make everyone else think they're tough so that no one will pick on them. It's all too complicated so I stop thinking and watch the kids talking across the tables.

A kid on my table tries to talk to me.

"Why're *you* here? I'm here because I lost it after my mom died of cancer."

I feel stripped naked by his honesty. I was about to make up an excuse but somehow his honesty leaves me with nowhere to go. I know what it feels like to lose your mom; I've lost mine even if she isn't dead... she might as well be, but although he's asked me why I'm here, I choose to ignore it...it's safer.

"I'm sorry for your loss. How long ago was it?"

He starts to tell me all about his mom dying and how he had nowhere to go and tried to kill himself because he felt so alone...that's what brought him to Beach Haven. He talks and talks, and I'm grateful. I'm intrigued that he's happy to talk so much, to reveal so much of himself, for I could never have done the same.

As he talks, though, I realize that this is what Miss Tina was talking about last night, sharing yourself and your stories. My stomach turns over and I wish I hadn't eaten so much. Can I do this? Can I share this much about myself with other people? I really don't know, and although a part of me is wincing with the raw honesty of it all, I feel bathed in it and I feel a sudden sense of safety, something I've never felt before, not like this.

I remember feeling safe in my mom's arms when we were together, just the two of us, but even then it wasn't the same as I'm feeling right this minute. Back then the sense of safety felt as if it were dependent upon me pleasing her, saying the right thing and always being there for her, whereas this doesn't feel anything like that...it just feels open, raw, honest and safe. I suddenly feel as if I can say anything and it will be okay, and the realization makes my breakfast churn in my stomach, so much so that I feel sick, but then Alison snatches my attention from me. She's staring at me, even though she's right over the other side of the dining room.

I flash her a brief smile, which hurts my smarting face, but she looks away. I feel crushed.

The kid, who tells me his name is Wayne, is still going on about his mom but I don't hear anything he says—I'm agitated yet too full to do anything about it. But if I weren't full up with second helpings of breakfast, what would I do with these feelings that are making my heart pound? I feel angry with Alison for looking down on me, for ignoring me, when I bothered to smile at her...I could have acted cool and ignored her...I wish I had. I'm mad at myself, and as anger flashes through me I snap at Wayne who's still going on about his mother dying.

"Well, I was only trying to make you feel welcome," he says, and pushes his chair away from the table, gets up, and walks over to the rest of the kids, leaving me alone.

I feel bad. I know I hurt his feelings but I couldn't help it, something flashed through me and I didn't know how to control it. Hell, this is too hard. I can't punch him because he hasn't done anything wrong; besides, I'd look pathetic in front of Alison and the others. Why am I so angry? I don't know, and I don't know what to do with my feelings.

Ken calls us all, telling us that it's time to clean our teeth and our rooms. I end up walking on my own with all the kids chattering ahead of me. The anger is still riding through me and I don't know why.

I scrub my teeth hard, my anger finding its way into my wrist and my toothbrush. I feel so misunderstood.

I stand at my window ignoring the shouts and laughter up and down the hall, and there in front of me is the ocean. I can't believe how powerful, yet how peaceful, it is. I open the window and I can smell the salt on the breeze—it's amazing—and seagulls are screeching outside my window, hovering in the wind. I hope we're allowed to go on the beach later.

"Okay, everyone, time for group," Ken yells down the hall, dragging me away from my thoughts.

I shut the window and follow the kids downstairs through a door with a sign above it that says "Group Room." It's a big room where kids are sitting around in a circle, and Miss Tina is sitting in an armchair waiting for everyone to settle down.

"Hi, everyone," she says, smiling at us all. "I'd like to welcome Shane."

She looks at me and I can feel my face going red. I feel scared, not the same fear as facing gang rape in juvenile, but scared nevertheless. Everyone's looking at me...some kids are smiling, others are staring and some are frowning. I can feel *something* flowing through me that is a mixture of anxiety and anger, and I don't know what to do with it. My palms are sweating. I can't wipe them on my sweats because the kids will see and know that I'm anxious, so I slide my hands under my thighs and sit on them, my teeth clenched.

"Shane, would you like to say why you're here?"

she asks.

No. I don't want to say why I'm here and suddenly all this feels too hard, and I think that right this minute I'd rather be in juvenile where I can act out and not have to face my behavior or my feelings.

Everyone's looking at me and suddenly I feel very hot...I don't know what to say or do, so I do nothing.

Kids start to look from me to Miss Tina and she says, "Shane, this is a safe place where everyone faces their behavior." She turns to the other kids and says, "We'll go around the room and each of you tell Shane why you're here, okay?"

I slide my hands back out from under my thighs, the sweat soaked up, and I put them under my armpits to contain their trembling, and to protect myself with my crossed arms. I listen to all the kids tell me why they're here...some say that they've been abused, others say they've run away from home because it was all too awful, others tell me that they're locked in a gang and can't get out because they're scared the gang members will kill their families. Several say that they tried to commit suicide because they couldn't cope anymore and they had no one to turn to, then finally it gets to be my turn and I suddenly don't feel so bad or scared that I will be judged.

"I'm here because the judge said I had to come so that I could work on my anger." I remember overhearing the guard tell that to the paramedics on the way to Beach Haven.

"Why're you angry?" Alison asks.

My tongue is instantly dry and I can barely talk.

"Um, well, um, because I got put in juvenile."

"Why, what d'you do?" a kid asks.

I cough and suddenly I feel like a bit of a jerk.

"It's okay for you to say," Miss Tina says, "Remember, this is a safe place."

I cough again. "I threatened to kill my stepfather."

"Why, what did he do?"

I don't know how to answer. How do I explain the awful creeping hatred that is between us? If I say it out loud it'll sound petty and stupid, but it's not, it's serious.

I feel instantly angry and I feel as if they're picking on me, trapping me to make me feel bad. All their faces are staring at me and all of a sudden it's too much, I can't cope with it, so I dart up from my seat and run from the room.

No one stops me and suddenly I feel stupid. I'll have to face them all in a while...how do I do that now and still save face? My heart is hammering and I'm desperate to get away from my feelings, so I open a door that leads out to a playground and head towards the beach.

The sand crunches beneath my feet as they sink and I wander a little way along the beach so that the staff and kids can't see me from the windows. I sit on the warm sand and watch the waves roll to within a few feet of me, my thoughts lost in a haze of agitation and anger. Seagulls are screeching above me and suddenly something wet splats on my hair and I know that one's just crapped on me. Well, that says it all, doesn't it? That just about describes me and my life; I sit here in all this wide-open space and still a seagull aims for my head and doesn't miss. If I thought that it would be hard to go back into the building and save face five minutes ago, how do I do it now that I've got seagull crap in my hair? I have no idea how to retract my exit and avoid being humiliated.

I'm so glad that I walked a little way from the building so that no one can see me because I gingerly creep down to the waterline and scoop seawater up, rubbing it into my hair to get rid of the mess...it's gross, but finally it's gone. Just in time too, because I turn when I hear voices. Wayne and a couple of kids walk towards me. I pray that my hair looks okay...I'll tell them I was hot, but they don't say anything so I don't either.

I stand there feeling awkward until they flop down onto the sand, so I do the same.

"I've been here two months," a boy who's older than me says, "Oh, my name's Ollie. Y'know, it's not so bad...most kids never want to leave here...I know I don't. It's hard to start with, though, because outside..." he waves his hand around, "hardly anyone is honest with each other, so at first it can be a bit of a shock having kids in your face telling you how it is."

Wayne nods and the other kid agrees.

"I felt like they were picking on me when I first came here, but I soon realized that they weren't, they were just being honest and asking me to be, too. I'm Liam, by the way."

My heart is beginning to slow down as I listen to them and my fear of being humiliated rolls away. I watch the surf roll back, leaving stranded soggy seaweed and bubbles of froth popping on the sand.

"Hi," I say, not knowing what to say. My anger's gone but in its place seems to be nothing...I've been angry for so long that I don't know how to *be* without it.

"We better be getting back," Wayne says, and they get up, brushing the sand from their jeans. I follow them, grateful to them for giving me a way back into the building where I'm not alone or humiliated, and no one seems to notice my wet hair or asks why it's wet.

There are kids everywhere, all talking at once, drinking soda and eating chips. We're in a big living room that's got squashy armchairs and sofas that once you sit in them it's hard to haul yourself out. I sit in one and a girl comes to sit next to me...it's not Alison, but she's nice anyway.

"Hi, I'm Josie. What happened to your face?"

"I got into a fight," I say with a hint of pride, which leaves me almost immediately when she frowns.

"Oh, what over?"

How can I tell her that I was afraid in juvenile; that a group of kids was going to get me? My face is red at the thought of it. A thought wanders into my mind, and I shake my head trying to get rid of it, but it doesn't go. When the police took me away in shackles from school, one of them ran his finger down my cheek and said, "Oh, you're a pretty boy, you'll be somebody's wife in jail if you don't shape up."

My stomach turns to jelly at the thought, especially as the image of the gang of naked boys in the shower is never far away, and I feel my hands tremble.

"What's the matter?" Josie asks, "You look dead pale."

"Nothin'," I snap.

She looks mad and goes to stand up but the sofa sucks her back down. I want to laugh but I can't because it all seems wrong and messed up. She's trying to get mad at me for snapping at her, I'm trying to shut her up so that she doesn't trigger scary images in my head. Yet all I want to do is talk to her and have her talk to me, but she's trying to storm off and can't. Why is everything so hard?

She eventually pulls herself out of the sofa and turns her back on me.

Miss Tina calls us and so I struggle to haul myself out of the sofa too and follow them back into the Group Room. I sit back into an armchair and pray that no one asks me anything...or even notices me.

"Today we're talking about anger and how to cope with it. Everyone gets angry; it's one of the core emotions," Miss Tina says.

I'm lost already. She stands up and goes towards a flip chart and starts drawing a picture of a dog's head.

"Now, this dog has a brain, just like every other mammal, and this part is called the brain stem, where the bodily functions are controlled. This part makes sure that the dog breathes, eats, drinks and sleeps, and also in this part of the brain are the four emotions that *every* mammal has. Who can tell me the four core emotions?"

A kid shoots up his hand and I immediately think "swot."

"Fear keeps company with mad, sad and glad."

Miss Tina smiles, "Yes, fear, anger, sadness and happiness. You will find those four emotions in an animal because they belong in the brain stem, which is the part of the brain that we all have in common with animals. If you look at a dog you can tell instantly if he's feeling fear, anger, sadness or happiness. All of you think of when you've seen your dog or cat show these emotions."

My cousin's got a dog and I've seen him growl

when he's angry, cower when he's scared, whine when he's sad and wag his tail when he's given a bone.

"Humans are no different because we share the same brain stem as all other mammals; it's only the thinking part of our brains that is different and what makes us human. So, if someone says, "Oh, I never get angry," they're lying. Everyone gets angry because it's part of being alive; it's what happens when we feel thwarted or frustrated, or powerless and helpless. Being angry is okay, it's a natural way to feel when things hurt us or when they go wrong, but it's how we express our anger that makes it positive or negative, and which ends up in positive or negative consequences."

She looks around the room and smiles.

"Let's look at how we express our anger." She holds out her pen. "Who wants to go first?"

"Is it how we express our anger now or how we used to?" a kid asks.

"Let's write how you used to behave and then we can compare how you deal with anger now, okay?"

Ollie goes first and writes, "fighting."

Josie writes, "pouting."

Wayne puts, "running away."

Liam writes, "punching my brother."

Alison writes, "playing my music really loud." She hands the pen to me and my stomach does a double flip.

I walk over to the flip chart and know that there's only one thing I can write with my face as beat-up as it is, and that's "fighting," but I want to write other things, like panic and crying.

One by one the rest of the kids add how they expressed their anger.

Smashing plates.

Slamming doors.

Tearing up books.

Someone writes "panic" and then someone writes, "cry," and I don't feel alone with my feelings anymore.

Cuss.

Spit.

Slap.

Scream at everyone.

Eat.

Get drunk.

Get high.

Hammering on doors.

Punch a hole in the wall.

Drive fast.

Hurt my little sister.

Kick the dog.

Throw up.

Lock myself in my room and refuse to come out.

Stay out all night.

Have sex.

Eat too much chocolate.

Go silent for days.

Bitch about the person who's made me angry so that they can hear.

Slash someone's tires.

Everyone is honest and even though some of the things they write are bad, very bad, we're all laughing in the end because it seems so stupid to behave that way just because we were angry.

Chapter Four

Miss Tina holds up her hands until we quiet down. "Now, did any of these behaviors solve any of the reasons for your anger?"

"No, but they sure felt good," a kid says, and I see Alison shake her head at him.

Some of the kids laugh but they soon go quiet when Miss Tina stands there looking serious. She says, "Yes, it may have felt good at the time, and the reason it did would have been because when you're angry tension in your body mounts and it has to *go* somewhere."

Everyone's quiet.

"When you get angry or scared, adrenaline starts flying around your body getting you prepared for action. Thousands of years ago when men were surrounded by dangerous animals that would eat them, the only defense the human body had was to be able to instantly get into a state where it could run away or fight...it was the way early man survived and is called the "fight or flight" response. That physiological response still lives within each of us even though we don't have to face man-eating animals anymore. When we get angry or scared, the body automatically triggers the production of adrenaline, which prepares the body to run or fight. It makes your heart pound, your head swim, your stomach feel sick, and your palms start sweating. The blood in your body is sent directly to your muscles and away from the brain, which accounts for why it's hard to think straight or rationally when you're angry or afraid. The tension these physiological responses bring about has to be released somehow and judging from your list..." she points with her pen..."this is how you've all released that tension in the past."

We're still quiet.

"But, my question to you all is, even though you may have released the tension in your bodies by behaving in these ways, did any one of them address the cause of your anger?"

I want to shout out "yes," because by fighting I got moved out of juvenile and away from the gang in the shower, but as I sit and think I realize that my anger is towards my mom and *him* and my aggressive behavior has done nothing to make the sense of betrayal I feel go away. It hasn't gotten rid of *him* either, in fact, now that I think about it, my aggression allowed him to get closer to my mom and push me further away. I see what she means; no, the way I dealt with my anger did nothing to address the cause of it.

I sit here listening to the others say much the same thing—how punching their younger brothers and sisters got them removed from the house and into foster care, how smashing walls, doors and plates did nothing but get them grounded, how driving fast got them a ticket and a ban from driving, how having sex got them a sexually transmitted disease, and drinking alcohol or getting high got them arrested and put on probation.

"I'm confused," says a kid. "If it's normal to release the tension in your body when you're angry or scared, then how come it's wrong?"

Miss Tina smiles at her.

"It's what you do to release the tension that is the key issue, and what the consequences are of the way you release that tension. Remember my favorite saying...

"Every behavior has a consequence,
Good behaviors have good consequences,
Bad behaviors have bad consequences,
So that means that I have the power over what
happens to me."

She turns the page over on the flip chart and writes down her favorite saying.

"Yes, you need to release the tension you feel when you're angry, but it's how you do it that makes all the difference. If you release that tension in a negative way, it will have negative consequences, which may mess up your life and do nothing to solve the reasons for your anger."

"That happened to me," Liam says. "I was so mad at my dad when he grounded me that, when my little brother got on my nerves, I pushed him and he fell down the stairs and broke his leg. That night I was in a foster home."

"Thanks, Liam," Miss Tina says. "So you were angry with your dad, you released the tension in your body by hitting your brother, and the consequence of that was very negative to you, and did nothing to sort out the problem between you and your dad...in fact, it made it worse."

Alison starts talking and I'm mesmerized. "I was really angry with my mom because she said that I couldn't go out on a date, so I went to my room and turned my music up so loud that the house vibrated."

"What happened?" Miss Tina asks.

"Dad took my music away and then I had to earn it back."

"So did your behavior do anything to solve the problem, did it enable you to compromise or negotiate with your parents so that you could go on the date?"

"No...it made it worse...I was grounded too, for cussing and being rude."

I think she's so cool and I hate the way my stomach churns with jealousy when she spoke of going on a date with some other guy.

"So, we have two things to consider when looking at anger; one, what to do with the tension it generates inside your body; and two, how to solve the problem that caused the sensation of anger. As the physiological response to anger is almost instant and knocks out your ability to think clearly, let's deal with that first."

I shift in my seat trying to take in everything she's saying and apply it to myself.

"What can you do that's physical to release the tension inside your body that won't harm yourself or anyone else, or break anything?"

"Go for a run."

"Work out."

"Chop wood."

"Scrub the bathroom."

"Dig the garden."

She smiles at us. "Yes, wonderful suggestions. Do you know that years ago I used to live in a four-story house, and that's a lot of stairs to clean. Any time I used to get mad I would vacuum the stairs from the top to the bottom of the house, and by the time I got down to the basement, the tension in my body had gone. I was no longer angry and as a bonus I was really pleased with myself because my house was clean. What other suggestions do you have to release the physical tension in your bodies when you're angry?"

"What about taking a shower or a bath?" Josie asks.

"Yes, you could do that. It's not the same vigorous exercise but it would allow you to relax, and that would release the tension."

"What about cycling?"

"Skateboarding."

"Track."

"Football."

"Basketball."

Miss Tina smiles. "Yes, all sports release tension."

"Punching a punch bag."

"Especially if it's got the person's face on it who's made you angry," Liam snickers.

"Now!" Miss Tina says, but smiles just the same.

I grin because I'd give anything to punch the hell out of a punch bag with *his* face on it. I'll have to ask for one at Christmas.

"Jumping Jacks."

"Okay, that's enough examples," Miss Tina says. "You've all got the point. When you're angry you need to find some safe way of releasing the tension that's built up in your bodies. When you've done that, you'll feel so much better and will be able to think more clearly. It's then that you will be able to talk about the problem or the reasons for your anger, and talking will help solve it."

"Alison, you said that you got angry because your mom wouldn't let you go on a date. Given that you're now calm having released the tension in your body, how could you have tackled the problem, which in your case was that your mom didn't want you to go on the date?"

I wince again and hate myself for doing so...what's wrong with me?

She shrugs. "I don't know. She'd already made up her mind that I wasn't going to go. Nothing I'd say would make her change her mind. It hurt because she made me feel like she didn't trust me."

"Hold up," Miss Tina says. "Let's think about it. After releasing the tension in your body that anger brings, it's time to think, to use your brains. The best way to negotiate a problem is to put yourself into another person's shoes."

She walks over to a stack of chairs and places two in the middle of the room.

"Okay, Alison, come and sit on one of these chairs." My stomach churns, wondering what's going to happen. I want to sit on the other chair next to her but of course I don't. I don't want all eyes on me, but yet I want to sit near her...what's happening to me? This is crazy.

Miss Tina says, "When you're sitting in this chair you are you, and when you're sitting in this chair opposite, you are your mom, okay? Now, ask your mom if you can go out on the date."

Alison starts acting.

"Mom, Ben's asked me out." (I suddenly hate the name Ben.) "Can I go, please?"

"Now, sit on your mom's seat and you *are* her, okay."

Alison's voice gets loud and higher.

"No, you can't. You're too young."

Miss Tina makes her sit back in the other chair so that she's herself again. "Now answer your mother."

"But all my friends go out on dates."

She sounds whiny.

She swaps chairs again and becomes her mom.

"I don't care what your friends are doing, you're too young and you're not going."

Alison stands up and stomps off towards the door, and then turns back grinning.

"That's when I went to my room and turned my music up as loud as it would go."

Miss Tina looks at us, and says, "So at that point you were mad, your mom was mad and both of you had a lot of tension that you needed to get rid of. It's tension that you have to get rid of on your own, for if you allow yourself to become tied up in a row, you'll say things that you'll regret and that'll make things worse. So what could you have done to get rid of the tension in your body?"

"I could have cleaned my room...it's a mess," she says with a small grin.

"Actually, that's a great idea," Miss Tina says, "for not only are you getting rid of the tension in your body but you're doing something that'll please your mother and lessen her tension. Nothing gets on a parent's nerves like a messy bedroom."

She's grinning and I grin, too, remembering how my mom always nagged me about my messy room.

"Okay, come back here, Alison."

She walks back to the two chairs in the middle of the room.

"So now your anger's spent and you can think clearly. Your mom's pleasantly surprised that you've cleaned your room without being nagged to death, so now is the moment that you try to understand what it feels like to be in her shoes."

"How?"

"Okay, be you and ask again but this time try and find out from your mom what she feels about you going on the date."

Alison sounds so grown up all of a sudden.

"Mom, Ben's asked me to go out with him and I want to go."

"Swap seats and become your mom."

She moves and doesn't grin at us, as she seems to be locked into a place where none of us exists any-more...there's just her and her mom.

"No, you can't, you're too young."

"Swap seats."

"Mom, I'm fourteen and I'm not going to do anything wrong. We're just going to go to a ballgame that his brother's playing in."

She jumps up again.

"No, I'm just trying to protect you. You're too young and I don't want anything to happen to you."

She's back in her seat again.

"I love you Mom, and I respect myself. I'm not going to do anything that'll make me lose respect for myself."

She gets up again and as she sits in the chair that is her mom, her voice changes and she seems calmer somehow.

"Okay, baby. It's not that I don't trust you; it's just that I'm scared and frightened for you. You can go but you have to be home by ten o'clock."

Silence hangs in the air and Alison looks stunned.

Miss Tina pats her back and smiles kindly at her.

"Was that different from how it happened?"

"Very."

"What are you feeling inside right this minute?" she asks Alison.

"I feel like crying because I handled it different-ly...I didn't get mad, and I think I understand why my mom said 'no' right away without explaining why. It's not that she's trying to ruin my fun, it's because she loves me so much and is scared for me."

Her voice breaks and I'm embarrassed, I don't know where to look...this is all too raw for me, I've never known anything like it. She's crying.

"Can I go and call my mom? I want to tell her I'm sorry."

"Of course."

She leaves the room and part of me wants to go with her, but another part wouldn't know what to say, so I sit here feeling a bit lost and stunned.

How could I have talked to my mom differently once the tension in my body caused by anger had gone away? My head's spinning. This is hard, much harder than juvenile. It's harder not to get angry and to face yourself.

When Alison comes back, she's smiling, and suddenly I feel better. Miss Tina tells her to sit back down.

"Alison, thank you so much for doing that. What did it feel like being your mom?"

"It was weird. I really felt as if I was her. I was able to see why she said "no," and I realized that she cares about me and was scared for me."

Miss Tina smiles at Alison as if she really loves her and then looks around at all of us.

"The purpose of doing that was to show you how to negotiate. Once you've released the tension the anger in your body causes, you can think straight. You can ask for what you want, explain why you want it, reassure others that you can be trusted and that you'll be safe. When you are able to do that, your parents will see you as an adult, with the ability to think as an adult, and you'll be far more likely to get your needs met if you behave this way than if you act out. Can you see?"

Someone hands Alison a tissue.

"Okay, this list of behaviors that you do to express your anger was before you came to Beach Haven. How do you express your anger now, after you've learned ways to get rid of the tension anger brings in your body?"

She turns over a clean page on the flip chart and starts to write as we call out.

"Count to ten."

"Talk, properly, like an adult."

"Walk away and wait until another day when things are calmer."

"Think like the other person so that you understand what they're thinking and feeling."

"Ask yourself why you get so angry so quickly," Alison says, and we all look at her.

"Indeed," Miss Tina says. "Well done, Alison. Do you get a lot of attention from your family by getting angry?"

There's a knock on the door...we all look up. It's Ken.

"Dinner time."

We file out of the room and head for the dining room, and I'm glad because my head's spinning with all that's happened this morning. It's a long way away from the shower in juvenile where I had to fight to save myself. Being here is *so* different and already I know what Miss Tina means about not having anyone here who fights or acts out because it would disrupt and unsettle everyone else. I felt so absorbed in what was going on between those two chairs with Alison and her invisible mother that to have someone in the group acting out would seem really out of place and wrong.

I eat less at dinner. Suddenly the need to fill myself is not so urgent, and I sit at the table, listening. I don't talk because I'm in awe of these kids who know so much more than I do, about life, about love, and about being honest.

I remember Miss Tina saying that in this place there were "no lies and no rescues," and suddenly I think I know what she means. No one can say things that aren't true about themselves because everyone else will see right through them. Each person has to accept his own truth without anyone else trying to reduce their discomfort by rescuing them. Hell, this is hard, too hard.

Ken calls us back; it's time to go back to the Group Room.

Miss Tina smiles at us as we take our seats again.

"Good dinner?"

"Okay."

"Right, listen up. You all worked really hard this morning so this afternoon I'm going to read a story that'll bring together everything we've learned, then after that you can sit on the beach or go swimming. Hey, no one said "swimming" as a way to release the tension in your body when you're angry...swimming's a great way."

I like swimming; how come I didn't think of it?

"Okay, are you ready?"

• • • •

Far, far away in the land that bobbed in and out of view depending upon the sea mist, a tribe lay dying, starving from lack of food.

"You must hunt further a field," the women said to their men, "or we will all die of starvation. Our children are hungry and we must feed them."

The men set off in different directions, some to go fishing upstream where the fish were thought to be, and others began a trek up into the tree covered mountains in search of deer.

Two hunters traveled far and wide across the plains until they reached the edge of a great forest, and they were about to cut through the brush when a fearful howl echoed through the trees.

"What's that?" one said to the other, shaking with fear.

"I don't know."

"I don't like it; what if it's a creature that's as hungry as we are?"

So reluctantly, because they were hungry and knew their people were relying on them, they began to cut their way through the forest, shivering each time they heard the howling. The bushes around them rustled.

"There's something there," the first man said, trembling and clinging to his friend, a scream poised on his lips. "We shouldn't have come, we'll be eaten, I just know it."

His friend, although he was sorely scared, shook him, saying, "Stop, we must listen and think."

They held on to each other for a moment as they tried to think, but as the bushes rustled even more, a scream shot out of their mouths. All of a sudden they were surrounded by tribesmen painted in war colors, each holding a brightly colored spear, with fear also resting upon their faces.

"Arrrhhhhh," they all cried together, as birds were startled from their nests.

It was a moment before each man stopped screaming and looked at each other, feeling suddenly foolish. They relaxed their spears, and before long the two hunters were sitting around a campfire with their new friends, eating chunks of freshly grilled wild boar.

"We heard a noise, a fearful noise," one of the hunters said to the chief, who glanced nervously around at his tribesmen.

"Yes, a truly fearful noise," said the other hunter. *"What was it?"*

The chief was silent for a moment but then the others around the fire nodded to him, saying, *"Tell them, perhaps they can help."* So he began to talk.

"Legend has it that long, long ago in the days of our forefathers each man was blessed with a gift called the 'feist,' a gift that kept him safe, a gift that was within him as his birthright. When saber tooth tigers roared and threatened to steal them from their beds, the 'feist' leaped to life warning them in time to run and hide, so that they could live in safety and not be eaten. But a great chill spread through the land, killing all the fearsome creatures and suddenly the 'feist' was no longer needed, for our people were safe and didn't need the god's gift of a rush that forced the body to be ready to fight in order to survive.

"As our people lived in peace the 'feist' lay dormant in every one of our forefathers until one, named Percy Qute, discovered a terrible truth...he learned by chance one day after dropping a stone on his toe that the 'feist' was ready and waiting to be called upon. As his toe smarted in pain, the 'feist' reared up inside him, making him roar with anger. He roared and roared until every member of the tribe, who had long since forgotten about the 'feist,' jumped up in fear. A terrible thing happened to Percy, for he saw the effect his 'feist' had upon those around him and he feasted upon his newfound

power, giving free-reign to the 'feist' within him.

"The children hid in terror, never having heard the roar of the 'feist' before, and seeing their mothers trembling they hid behind their skirts. Their fathers cowered beneath Percy's 'feist' not knowing what to do, for in their lifetime all the tribesmen were calm and were able to see, to understand and to negotiate with each other. They suddenly didn't know what to do. Some, watching how Percy Qute enjoyed the power he had over other people, were just about to copy Percy Qute's roaring when they noticed something terrible happening to him. Every time he roared and gave free-reign to the 'feist' within him—which, remember, was a gift from the gods in the days when saber tooth tigers roamed the forest—hairs began to sprout from his body.

"Percy was so shocked and afraid as the 'feist' roared through him and hair sprouted all over his body, that his fear caused him to roar even louder and harder. But as he did so more hair grew from his body until he looked like a caveman with large bushy eyebrows that obscured his vision.

"As the cowering children came out from behind their mothers' skirts, they laughed. Little by little the laughter rippled through the crowd, and those who had been tempted to follow Percy Qute and display the 'feist' that was dormant within each of them let the 'feist' flow out of them and they laughed along with their children.

"Percy Qute, dumbfounded by the tribesfolk laughing at his rage when he was accustomed to its power over everyone else, stumbled blindly away from their scornful laughter, heading for the forest and the sanctuary of the trees."

The two hunters sat around the campfire, their mouths open and eyes wide, fear resting in their hearts.

"What happened to Percy Qute?" one whispered.

"Legend tells us that Percy Qute still lives in the forest, blinded forever by his rage, for as he roars and misuses the 'feist,' he becomes more and more like an animal. They say that the terrible blood-curdling roar that rages through the trees is Percy ravaged by anger, by the 'feist' that no longer is the gift that the gods intended it to be."

The hunters looked at each other fearfully.

"The noise...it was him?" They shook as the realization dawned on them. "He still lives in the forest?"

The tribesmen were silent around the campfire, glancing at each other, no one wanting to break the silence, yet the stillness answered the hunters' question.

"The noise we heard, was it him?" they asked again.

"Tell them," a wisened old woman demanded.

The tribesmen glanced at each other again and

then the chief spoke.

"Yes, it's him. He still lives, driven by the 'feist,' his anger, his rage, and yet in allowing himself to be so angry his hair grows, his eyebrows lengthen and his blindness is complete. He's allowed the 'feist' to take over his body and mind so his hair grows and his eyebrows completely cover his eyes, therefore he can see nothing and understand nothing."

Sparks burst from the campfire into the air and all those around it fell silent for a moment until the chief spoke again.

"If you will help us be rid of Percy Qute's roar and his awful howling, which frightens our children so much, we will give you deer meat forevermore so that your people won't go hungry ever again."

The two hunters looked at each other, fear alive in their faces, for neither relished the thought of coming face to face with someone driven by the 'feist,' but the thought of their own people, starving and desperate, gave them a little strength.

"O...o...okay, we'll help you, if we can."

The next day, after a breakfast of deer and yams, the two hunters set off with the elders of the tribe, their arrows and knives at the ready. They forged a path deep into the forest, following the roar they knew to belong to Percy Qute, who was blinded and angry, and they tracked him all day, scared, their own 'feist' longing to be heard.

That night deep within the forest, Percy's roar

echoed through the trees and they sat around their fire roasting hedgehogs and grubs, hungry, yet fearful.

"How are we going to do this?" the older hunter asked. "We need to think about it. We can't just rush in there and make an angry, aggressive noise; we have to work out what to do. C'mon, let's use the brains the gods have given us."

The second hunter sat for a moment stroking his beard.

"You said that Percy Qute lost the ability to be able to see clearly, to think and to negotiate after he allowed the 'feist' free reign to control him, and in doing so his hair grew so much that his eyebrows stopped him from being able to see everything that you can see and understand."

"Yes, that's right," said the chief.

"Well, what we need to do is to enable him to see."

"How?"

The hunter sat and thought for a moment, glad that it was dark and that no one could see his indecision.

"Well, if we can creep up on him while he's asleep and cut off his eyebrows, then when he wakes he'll be able to see, I mean, to really see. Then he'll have no need to let the 'feist' flow through him and blind him."

"That's a great idea," said the chief, and he immediately poured water on the fire and ordered his people to follow him into the depth of the forest to creep up on the sleeping Percy Qute.

It was remarkably easy to find Percy, whose snores were like an angry thunderstorm, and as they tip-toed carefully around him, not daring to breathe, the hunters took out their knives.

Within seconds the thick heavy eyebrows were cropped from Percy Qute's face leaving his eyes, that had not seen reason for eons, alive and curious. They slipped away as he stirred, hiding behind a bush, praying that his rage, the 'feist,' would somehow be silenced by the new truths before him when he opened his eyes and saw—really saw—that there was no reason to be angry all the time.

They didn't have long to wait, for within minutes, as the sun began to rise, Percy Qute opened his eyes and immediately shielded them with his hands, and the hunters and tribesmen knew that he could see. Not one dared to take a deep breath; most had their hands clamped over their mouths.

Percy sat up, stunned, looking around him. His roar, now muted, was gone, having no purpose, for he had the gift of sight, the gift of insight, so the gift of the 'feist' was now redundant.

He sat there dumbfounded and silent.

The trees rested and swayed in the breeze, no longer shaken by the rage of Percy Qute and his 'feist,' and the howling that had terrified the tribesmen and their families stopped. Percy, now that he did not intimidate or frighten those around him, left to seek his fortune and to start again, knowing that anger would never really get him what he wanted, while the tribesmen and the two hunters returned to the village to celebrate.

The chief kept his word and sent deer meat to the hunters' tribe every week, and so from that day forth the hunters' families thrived. The tribesmen also thrived in the knowledge that the gift of the 'feist' was a gift from ages gone by, but in the present the gods gave another gift, that of understanding and negotiation, the gift the gods intended for their people right now, in this age. And so the people lived with their dormant 'feist' and learned how to control it, and although it was hard they learned how to use the changing gifts from the gods, the gifts of understanding and negotiation in an age where fighting was no longer necessary to survive.

Chapter Five

"**C**an you see what the story's about?" Miss Tina asks us. "The 'feist' is the adrenaline in our bodies that in cavemen days helped human beings survive...anger and fear had a function and were useful, but now it's not necessary in the same way that it was thousands of years ago and now it causes humans a problem."

"Why did Percy's hair grow so fast?" a kid asks.

Miss Tina grins at us. "The idea of becoming very hairy was to illustrate how like an animal we become if we allow raw anger and aggression to control us." She laughs, "And the idea of making his eyebrows become so long that he couldn't see made me laugh, but more importantly it was to illustrate that if we allow ourselves to be controlled by anger, we fail to *see*. We fail to understand or to think clearly so that we can see what's really going on. Anger and aggression stop us from being able to think or solve our problems."

"So, is anger wrong then?" Wayne asks.

"No, it's not wrong, being angry is okay, it's a natural way to feel when things hurt us or when they go wrong, but it's how we express that anger that makes it positive or negative, okay or not okay," Miss Tina says.

She walks over to the flip chart again and turns to the page with all our new ways of dealing with anger.

"We looked at all the different ways to deal with the tension inside you when you get angry and most of those ways were physical, but what about ways that are not physical, what about ways that only involve thinking, thought techniques?"

I frown.

"There are ways of dealing with anger that are not physical, and counting to ten is one way. Who can think of why these ways would help you calm down?"

Alison calls out, "Because thinking takes your mind off the reason for your anger."

"Well, yes, that's partially why, but it's a little more complicated than that. We've already learned that if you get really angry, you stop thinking clearly, so if you force yourself to think about something else your brain will attend to it and will be diverted from the reasons why you're angry. Not only will your brain then focus upon something else, but in the act of doing so your diverted thoughts will act upon your hormones, and that will change the way you feel. In other words, the way you think affects your feelings, which in turn affects your behavior."

Ollie says, "I always play my music really loud through my head phones when I'm mad and it takes my mind off it."

"Not too loud, I hope, we don't want you to go deaf," Miss Tina says, smiling. "Can you see, though, that by listening to your music you are forcing your brain to focus upon something else other than the reasons for your anger?"

He nods.

"How do you feel when you listen to music?"

"Good...it takes me to a cool place," he grins, and some kids nod.

"That's how I feel when I listen to music," Alison says. "That's why it was so awful when my dad took my music away."

Some kids agree with her around the room and I know what she means because I'd go crazy without my music. Miss Tina holds up her hand to silence us.

"We can train our brains to react in a certain way when we're angry...it's called 'guided imagery.' It takes a little practice but it works every time and it can be fun."

"Can I use the bathroom?" Josie asks.

"Yes, let's stop for a while and have a break," Miss Tina says.

I'm glad because my head is spinning with everything that we've done today. My body is still smarting but as I've listened to everything that's happened in the Group Room, I've been more focused upon that than the pain in my body. As I line up to get a soda I realize that's what Miss Tina is talking about; you can train your mind to focus upon one thing and not another. My brain was focused upon what was going on in the group, and upon Alison, so that I wasn't focused upon the pain in my body...that's the same as focusing my brain upon something else other than my anger.

I get my soda and Ken calls me.

"Hey, Shane, come here, man."

I walk out of the room and there in front of me is my mom and *him*. My heart seems to stop for a moment and then begins to race.

"Shane," she says, with something in her voice that I can't quite place, and then I see his face, a pace behind her so that she can't see him...he is grinning at me and instantly anger is darting through me. My heart is pounding and I feel such hatred towards him that I think my chest might burst. I barely hear my mom.

"Shane, I've brought your clothes. Are you all right? I've been so worried."

Something terrible is happening inside my heart... it feels as if something has just grabbed it and is squeezing the life out of it...the pain is terrible. She walks towards me, almost at a run, but *he* takes her arm and holds her back, away from me, and I hate him even more than I thought was possible. There's something painful in her face, which I ignore, for the only thing that I can see is the leer on his face.

I charge at him.

"Get off her," I scream, suddenly demented. "Let her go."

She starts to say "shhh" and looks frightened, but I won't shut up. It's the smile on his face that makes me crazy. He knows what he's doing, he always has and yet no one will believe me. Ever since my mom met him, he's been trying to separate us; he just can't stand it that my mom and I are close. Yet as these thoughts flash into my head, they immediately fly away for my anger is so raw that I can't think of anything other than to smash his face in, so I lunge at him.

It happens so fast that I don't really take it all in. Someone grabs me firmly but gently at the same time. There's shouting and it's coming from me as I'm pulled away, but I can't stop even though I know that all the kids are standing around in the hall, watching, for the only thing that filters through my rage is the leer on *his* face.

I'm cussing badly, unable to stop, and suddenly I find myself in a room with Ken leaning against the door, inside with me, panting.

"Hey man, are you determined that I'm going to earn my money? Calm down, okay?"

Something is flying through me that stops me from calming down...I want to kill *him*. He knows what he's doing and no one seems to see it except me. As I flop down onto a bed in the corner of the room my blood rages through me. I'm so mad that my heart is pounding, yet as I lie there facing away from Ken, who's still panting, I feel tears spring into my eyes.

Damn it, I can't help it, I start crying. This is all too hard. I don't know what's happening to me...one minute I'm okay and the next minute I feel as if every ounce of sanity is seeping out of me, and in its place creeps a hideous sense of sadness, of grief.

In this moment I hate myself for I cry like a baby. I'm so glad that none of the kids can see me, although that doesn't stop me from feeling humiliated knowing that Ken's in the room, but he makes it okay.

"I know what you're going through, Shane, my stepdad did the same to me and it was ages before my mom saw sense and left him. But she *did* leave and so we were able to mend our relationship. Man, it was painful, but it worked out. Try and think about all those kids whose moms never come to their senses; they're stuck with a man in their lives that they never asked for, and then they suffer the sense of being pushed aside by someone who will stop at nothing to break the bond between mother and child. I know what it was like and I see it all the time, so I know what you're going through, okay?"

I hear him, but just barely, as my "feist" is still raging through my body at the injustice of it all. But as my heart slows I allow myself to listen and to think about what Miss Tina said about not being able to think straight when you're angry. While I was so angry I couldn't think straight, yet as the "feist" leaves me and I calm down, I can begin to think. Already I'm not thinking about *him* and am trying to work out how to apply the things Miss Tina told us to my situation. I think I understand what she means. Think about something other than the thing that made you mad and you'll calm down, then you can think clearly.

"Are you ready to get out of here?" Ken asks gently.

I nod, not trusting my voice, which is likely to break.

"C'mon then, let's go and join the others."

I find my voice, which is shaky.

"No, I can't."

I can't let the kids see that I've been crying, and also knowing how Miss Tina feels about fighting and aggression, I feel ashamed of myself...not because I care about *him*, I don't, but because I'm ashamed of my anger in front of the other kids and after Miss Tina trusted me.

"Listen, Shane, this is a safe place and facing our thoughts, feelings and behaviors is what we do here. So come on, let's go."

He doesn't wait for an answer or give me the opportunity to rebel, so I follow him, reluctantly, my face very red and my body spent.

No one seems to say anything at first when Ken and I go back into the Group Room, where all the kids are already seated. I sit down.

"Now, as I was saying," Miss Tina starts, "we can train our brains to react in a certain way when we're angry...it's called 'guided imagery.' It takes a little practice but it works every time and it can be fun. When something or someone makes you really mad, you can force your mind to make it go away by imagining different scenes and enacting them."

My heart is racing so fast that I barely hear her, and I'm vaguely aware that the kids keep glancing at me.

She looks right at me and I shrivel beneath her gaze.

"Shane, come here," she says, pointing to a chair next to where she's standing.

I want to run from the room, but I can't. I can't do that twice in one day and expect these kids, who seem to be so much more truthful than I am, to respect me, so I get up with my stomach in shreds, walk over to her and sit down by her side. Something weird comes over me; she's so close to me that suddenly I feel safe and I know that no one will hurt me while she's around. She makes it okay, even though I'm scared inside.

"Shane, you just got mad at your mom. Try to explain what was happening inside you and we'll work through what happened, how *you* were feeling and also what your mom and stepdad were feeling, then how you could have dealt with it differently."

Everyone's looking at me and I feel terrible.

"I wasn't angry with my mom, I was angry with my stepfather."

"What did you feel before you rushed towards him?" she asks.

"Angry. He was laughing at me, he always does, and when my mom went to walk towards me, he stopped her. Ever since she met him he's done his best to split us up, he can't stand it that we're close... I mean, we *were* close."

I can feel my hands trembling and I'm terrified that I'm about to cry again.

Miss Tina looks at me.

"It sounds to me as if you *are* very close, not *were*. What do you think she was feeling when she saw you?"

Something shifts inside me as I think of the two chairs that Alison sat in while being herself and then her mom, and suddenly I know what my mom was thinking. My heart wrenches painfully and I swallow hard, but nothing stops the tears from falling down my face as I recognize that the love I thought had gone between my mom and me is still painfully alive. I can't think straight again, although I'm not angry, for something is going on inside my body. I can feel my heart pounding and I feel sick and sweaty. I try to look away from the kids who are all staring at me but there's nowhere to look where they can't see me, so I stare at my feet and don't look back at them.

"What do you think your mom was feeling when she saw you?" Miss Tina asks again, pressing me to answer.

"I don't know," I sniff. "She misses me, she's scared for me..."

"And?"

I whisper, "She probably feels guilty because she can't stand up to him."

"I think you're right," she says. "What d'you think your stepfather was thinking?"

My tears stop when she mentions him.

"Jealousy and hatred," I say, knowing that I'm right. "He wants me out of the way and will do anything he can to make sure it happens."

Miss Tina hands me a box of tissues and I blow my nose noisily.

"Everything you say may be right but, you know, we cannot change other people; the only person we can change is ourselves and hope that others will then interact with us in a different way because we've behaved differently. So, with that in mind, Shane, what can you do differently that will stop you from feeling so manipulated and hurt by your stepfather?"

I shrug, for I really don't know what I could do differently, because I'm so bogged down with my hatred towards him and my anger towards my mom for not standing up to him.

Miss Tina looks at the kids and asks them.

"What could Shane do differently that would stop him from feeling so manipulated and hurt by his stepfather?"

"Ignore him."

"Be mega good so that he hasn't got a reason to pick on Shane."

"Don't try and be extra close to your mom while he's around if he's that jealous."

"Punch him," a kid says, but when Miss Tina shoots him a glance that tells him to be quiet, he looks down.

"Try and talk to him."

I shake my head because everything they're saying won't work, I know it won't. He doesn't want things to be right in our house...all he wants is for me to go and for him to have my mom all for himself.

"Tell a social worker or school counselor what's going on and let them help."

"Yeah, really," I think, "he'll just pick on me more if he thinks I've told someone outside the house, but worse than that, he'll pick on my mom and I can't let that happen."

"Be nice to him, perhaps he's jealous for a reason, perhaps you and your mom really are too close and maybe he feels left out," Alison says.

I feel my "feist" flare inside me when she says that, and I can feel my jaw clench.

We all sit in silence for a moment, thinking. Miss Tina then says, "Y'know, all the things you've suggested may work, but they may not. They all imply that the child has to do the 'fixing' of the things that are wrong in the family. That often happens and really it shouldn't. Adults are supposed to be adults, in charge and reasonable. You can try all those things, Shane, except punching," she frowns at the kid who suggested it, "and none of them will hurt the situation. But if none of those suggestions works, then what you need to do is to make sure you are safe from your stepfather's taunting, and that's where 'guided imagery' comes in useful."

"You've all seen those glass domes with a Christmas scene inside them, and when you turn them upside down it snows or has sparkles that fall as snow, right? Okay, well this piece of 'guided imagery' uses them. Are you ready, Shane? I want you to shut your eyes and listen. Listen really closely and let yourself flow with the things I'm going to suggest."

I can feel my breathing slowing and I don't feel so agitated anymore, even though we've just been talking about the person I hate the most in my life. Miss Tina's voice becomes soft and gentle and I'm drawn to listening to her and nothing else.

"I want you to imagine your most favorite place in the world...think about it now...how it looks and how it smells. What does it feel like standing in that place? Think about it and be there in your head."

I know where my favorite place was...it was before Mom met *him*, when we lived in our old house. My granddad had made me a tree house when I was little and I can still remember him climbing up the old oak tree in our back yard dressed in his work overalls, with nails in his mouth and a hammer sticking out of his pocket. Mom didn't want me to help as she said that I was too little, but Granddad lifted me into the tree and I held the nails so that he could talk to me.

We had a party in the treehouse once it was finished and all my friends came...it was so cool. There were always kids coming to my house so that they could play in it, but as I got older it became a place where I could go to be alone when I wanted to think, or when I wanted to listen to my music on my headphones and not have to do my chores.

"Think about that place," Miss Tina says gently. "What does it feel like, what can you see, what can you smell, what can you hear?"

I can smell the leaves of the tree, which rustle outside the door when the wind blows. I hear them scraping against the walls and the floor and I can smell the freshly cut grass beneath me. I can hear the bubbles popping in my glass of soda that rests on the shelf Granddad built just inside the door. There's a breeze wafting over my face coming through the windows as a storm brews outside stirring up the tree, its branches and its leaves.

"Now imagine that your special place is the scene inside one of those snowstorm domes. See your special place in the center of the floor and the glass dome rising high above it, encasing you within your special place. Feel how safe that feels with the glass dome above you...nothing can get in, nothing. You can see out and watch what's happening outside your special safe place but nothing nasty can get inside to hurt you. There's a tiny locked trapdoor in the floor of the dome and only you have the key. Clench your fist around the key so that it's safe."

I tighten my fist, and as I listen to her it really feels as if there's a tiny key in my closed hand.

"That means that you can let who you like in but keep everyone else out as you're in charge of the key. Only *you* can let people into your safe place if and when you want to, and no matter what anyone else does outside your dome they cannot enter your safe place."

I feel very drowsy and I'm not sure how long I've been sitting on the chair in front of the group, but gradually I'm aware of the kids coughing and scraping their chairs. I feel very calm and it feels amazing.

"I did it, too," Alison says.

"Me, too," several others say.

"Good. The whole purpose of this exercise is to give you a safe place to go to when things get tough. It's a place where you're in charge and no one can enter or can hurt you," Miss Tina says, looking pleased.

"Shane, I want you to think of your safe place and be there, safely under the dome, okay?"

"Yes, I'm there," I say, finding it very easy to imagine myself back in the sanctuary of my tree house.

"Okay, now look out at the clear walls of the dome and see your stepfather...he's laughing at you."

I can feel my heart begin to hammer.

Miss Tina talks over my discomfort, though. "Look at him...he's trying to get to you, trying to goad you, to instigate you, but no matter how hard he tries he can't get through the dome wall. You're safe from him; he can't do anything to hurt you and you have no need to react to his behavior. Just look around your safe place and feel what it's like to be there, safe from everything that hurts you or upsets you."

In my head I see *his* face, laughing at me as he's done so many times before, but my heart rate stays steady, and I allow myself to savor everything about my safe place beneath the glass dome in my head. I see him hammering on the glass in frustration, his leer gone. He's suddenly powerless. He can do what he likes to try and instigate me, but I'm safe inside my dome, my own private safe haven. A thought flashes into my head. Now I know why this place is called Beach Haven—a haven is a place where you can rest safely, where others can't hurt you.

My heart is beating calmly and I feel great.

Alison says, "Wow, Miss Tina, I feel really good. I feel as if I can keep myself safe when my uncle starts picking on me now. It almost feels like I have a secret that they can't ever know about."

She's smiling and she looks like a kid at Christmas.

Other kids are nodding and agreeing.

"It's amazing, isn't it?" Miss Tina says. "Who would think that each of us has the power to be able to use our brains to control our anger and to be able to keep ourselves safe? My favorite image is to picture myself sitting in a beautiful garden in my hometown...it's a place that used to be an old hospital where people went to die...it scared me as a kid. But when it became rundown, it was turned into the most wonderful garden I've ever seen. Y'know, if you can imagine being in such a place, it's very difficult for anyone to intrude. Not only are you very calm, which means you're less likely to respond to someone instigating you, but you'll give that person the message that he may as well give up because he's not going to get through to you or be able to goad you."

She tells me to go back to my chair in the group and doesn't say one word about me losing my temper and being aggressive in Beach Haven, which I know is not allowed. I'm so grateful that she's given me another chance.

"Okay, so we've talked about 'guided imagery' as a way of keeping yourself safe from others who try to instigate you and make you angry, but what happens if you're already angry? What 'guided imagery' can you use to get rid of the anger that's already flowing through your body?"

We all look at her waiting for the answer.

"Someone wrote on the flipchart that taking a hot bath was a good way to get rid of anger, and although it isn't a physical activity—which is almost always the best way to get rid of the tension in your bodies that builds up when you're angry—it is a good way of relaxing. I've got another good piece of 'guided imagery' that will help you. When you're angry and the 'feist' is raging through you, not only will your heart beat very fast but you'll also start sweating. I want each of you to close your eyes."

I close mine and listen.

"I want you to 'see' the beads of sweat glistening on your body; they are Anger Beads. Within each bead the reason for your anger floats, turning the bead a mucky dirty color. Imagine that your body is covered in these Anger Beads, and as they get too full of anger they burst, leaving your skin covered in mucky Anger Slime."

Ugh, my body's covered in mucky slime, all originating from my anger towards *him*, and I know exactly what I have to do.

"The only way to get rid of the Anger Beads covering your body, and those that have already burst leaving you covered in mucky Anger Slime, is to have a shower and scrub them off. As you stand beneath the water I want you to 'see' the Anger Beads drop away from you and roll down the drain. If your anger's so bad that the Anger Beads burst and you're covered in mucky Anger Slime, then scrub your body good and hard and 'see' all the Anger Slime disappear down the drain."

I suddenly feel very itchy and dirty, and I long to take a shower.

"Open your eyes," Miss Tina says.

I look around and every one of us looks disgusted.

Miss Tina starts to laugh as she watches our faces, then we laugh too.

"It's pretty gross, isn't it? But it really is a great piece of 'guided imagery,' for what better way of getting rid of anger than to wash it down the drain. You'll feel free of it and clean. Try it."

"I feel filthy," I say. "My anger towards my stepfather has burst all over me and I need to take a shower."

"Me too," most of the kids say over each other.

Miss Tina's laughing.

"Okay, you've all worked really hard today. We've learned about where anger comes from and that it's a normal response to things that hurt us, or things that go wrong in our lives. Then we've learned how to cope with anger using physical activities to release the tension inside your body that builds when you get angry, so that you won't get into trouble by acting out your anger. Then we've learned some mental techniques, 'guided imagery' to help you stay safe and resist other people's instigation, and then to help you get rid of your anger by washing it away.

"Yes," she laughs, "I imagine that you all feel mucky with Anger Slime; go and shower, all of you. Get rid of your anger and feel clean."

We all rush out of the room and race up the stairs to our rooms. I can't wait to stand beneath the steaming water and watch my Anger Beads disappear down the drain, and to scrub myself clean of mucky Anger Slime...cool.

Chapter Six

I scrub and scrub myself imagining all the Anger Slime sliding down the drain and *him* with it. I feel good, not only clean, but good.

I come out of my room and follow the other kids downstairs.

"We get to make our own dinner tonight," Ollie says, as we go into a classroom that has lots of ovens and sinks set out like several little kitchens around the room. "That's Miss Cassie; she's our Life Skills teacher. She's cool."

There's a huge table at one end of the classroom and she asks all of us to sit down while she pulls her chair out and sits at the head of it.

"Today we're going to make pizza," she says, and some of the kids cheer. She holds her hand up to silence us, and grins. "D'you know, there's never a time when I don't want to eat pizza, but it's not only good to eat, it tells us a story too, a story about life. I think life is like a pizza. Can anyone think why?"

"Because it's a mess?"

She laughs. "It can be, yep, life can be messy and so can a pizza, but let's think about it. Today each one of you is going to be a chef, the one who decides what kind of pizza he wants to make, just as you are the one that decides what kind of life you will have."

She stands up and walks around the table putting something in front of each of us. Alison gets an onion, Liam gets a clove of garlic, I get a red pepper, Wayne gets a tin of stuffed green olives, and there's a big bag of pizza dough, a chunk of cheese, tomatoes, shrimp, sausage, pepperoni, a tin of anchovies, a bag of mushrooms, two bundles of spring onions, and a pot of salt and pepper. Then she puts all manner of pots and pans in the middle of the table, with lots of little bowls and silverware.

As she sits back down she picks up one of the pizza trays and holds it up in front of her.

"Think of your life as a pizza."

We frown, but she carries on.

"Think of your life as a pizza. You have to make it fit the pan because if it doesn't then it won't be right—it'll burn, fall apart and be in pieces—so that means that you have to fit into this world, the world is your pan. Do you understand? In this case the pizza pan is the world, where human beings have to fit.

"If we see the pizza as a human life, then how tasty, satisfying and nourishing your life will be will depend upon the amount of effort you put into making it. How your life turns out, how satisfying and how good it becomes, is going to depend on how much care you take and what you choose to do with it, just like your pizza."

She uses weighing scales and gives us each a dollop of dough and tells us to knead it with our fingers. I laugh as Alison has flour on her nose and she glares at me.

It feels squashy under my fingers. I've never made pizza before; it's fun.

Miss Cassie stands at the head of the table and she has three lumps of dough in front of her. She lifts one piece up.

"Okay, so I'm the chef, the one with free will, the one that will decide on how my pizza is going to be made. The piece you hold is your life," she says again. "What are you going to do with it? Are you going to treat it right? Are you going to take care of it or drop it on the floor so that it gets dirt in it and makes you sick? Are you going to treat it with care and roll it out to make the right shape, or if you can't be bothered are you going to take so little care that it's going to be a mess? Or are you just going to squash it and see how it turns out?"

She takes a rolling pin and before our eyes she rolls lightly and turns her dough as she rolls it, making a perfect round shape, then she moves to the next lump of dough and rolls the pin unevenly and carelessly, so that it's lumpy and shaped like a lopsided cloud. Then she makes us all jump as she slams the heel of her hand down on to the third lump of dough, bashing it this way and that until it's squashed flat.

"What do you think?" she asks. "Look at these three pizza bases, these three lives. We are the chefs, or the master of our lives. The chef that made this pizza cares about his life," she points to the first perfect shape, "but this person doesn't care too much about making his life as good as it could be," she points to the lopsided shape. "And this person has deliberately not bothered to try and make his life good, in fact, it looks like this person has deliberately tried to destroy it when it could have been great."

I ask myself, "Am I the last chef? Have I deliberately tried to mess up my life when it could be great?"

"And all this before we even start putting all the good things on our pizzas to make them good and nourishing, or rather, and all this before we even begin to fill our lives with good things that will make us happy and good people."

We're all quiet for a moment until Miss Cassie tells us to roll out our dough to fit the size of our pizza tray. I try hard to get it to be as round as I can, but I seem to have grown too many fingers and the dough has a mind of its own. I glance at Ollie and I can see him squashing the edges out with his thumbs, trying to make it fit. He's cussing under his breath and I grin.

When we stop kneading and rolling Miss Cassie starts talking again.

"Are you satisfied with your pizzas? And I want you all to think about whether you're satisfied with your lives."

Most of the kids mutter "no."

"Okay, now to prepare for what you're going to put on your pizzas, what you're going to put in your lives. Let's each prepare one thing and put it in one of the bowls in the middle of the table, and when it's all ready we can choose. Remember, you're the chef, you get to choose what's going on your pizza, just as you get to choose what you do in your life."

We all start chopping, grating and peeling. Alison's got tears pouring down her face from chopping the onion and Liam's teeth are clenched together as he squeezes the garlic cloves through the mincer. I'm staring at the red pepper and feel stupid. I have no idea what to do with it but Miss Cassie comes over and shows me what to do. It's hollow inside with lots of seeds, but soon it's sliced into thin slithers and placed in one of the bowls.

"How am I supposed to peel these mushrooms?" a kid asks. "They keep breaking away from their stalks; it's too hard."

"Ah," Miss Cassie says, smiling. "No one said that what you choose to put in your lives would be easy."

Eventually we wash our hands and all sit around the table with our pizza bases ready and lots of bowls with things to choose from to go on top of them in front of us.

"Right, before we go any further, we need to do something else first."

She stands up and walks around the table giving each of us a plain white label.

"We've got lots of yummy things to put on our pizzas but we need to name all the good things that we can put in our lives. I'll start, okay?"

She thinks for a moment and says, "I want children in my life," so she writes "children" on the label and sticks it next to the bowl of mushrooms.

She passes the pencil to Alison and asks, "What is it that you want in your life?"

Alison writes, "to have a home," and sticks the label by a bowl of sliced pepperoni. I know what I want in my life; I write, "to live happily with my mom without my stepdad" on my label, then I stick my label next to the bowl of peppers I've just sliced.

Everyone writes a label and they say what they want in their lives. The labels say a new car, to be a pop star, to have a boyfriend, to have a girlfriend, to have no nightmares, to get an education, to have friends, to have a proper family, to go to college, to get a basketball scholarship, to be happy, to believe in something, to be loved.

We're all pretty quiet as each kid sticks their label by the bowl of food they prepared.

Miss Cassie smiles at us. "Good job. Now, remember, you're the chef. You're going to make your pizza for dinner and you get to choose what toppings you put on it, and as you do I want you to remind yourself that you are the person that's in charge of your choices. As you choose what goes on your pizza, think about the things you choose to have in your lives. What is it that you want? For you are in charge of your lives—they're yours to live, yours to make as good as possible."

We all get up from our chairs and it's noisy, yet I'm deep in thought. I want my mom in my life, the mom I used to know before she got married to *him*, before she changed into someone who can't stand up for herself, or for me. I don't want *him* in my life. As I put bits of chopped up food on my pizza base the thought flashes through my head that if she won't give him up and I don't want him in my life, that means that I won't be able to live with them anymore. That means that I won't have my mom anymore. I suddenly feel sick and not at all hungry.

When we've finished putting food on our pizza dough, Miss Cassie tells us all to sit down again.

"Now, look at your pizza. How much care did you

take? Did you just throw it all on or did you put each piece of food carefully in the place where you felt that it was supposed to go? Your pizza is your life; have you taken care with it so that it's the best that it can be, the best that you can make it?"

I look at mine and feel a bit ashamed, since while I was thinking about my life, I didn't take as much care as I could have. I can feel my cheeks burning when a thought hits me...I didn't take enough care in my life, and I ended up in juvenile.

I glance over at Ollie's and see that the things he chose are clumped together and slopped over the side of the pizza tray.

Miss Cassie says, "There's one final thing to do and that is to bake it, and what I mean by that is to 'live your life,' and how will you do that? Will you shove it in the oven, walk away and not tend to it, leaving it to scorch or burn? Or will you keep an eye on it, make adjustments to it if you think it might get ruined, so that it'll turn out right? Think about it, what are *you* going to do to make your life as good as it possibly can be?"

She looks at each of our pizzas and says "good job" to most of us but when she gets to Ollie she says, "Oh, dear. You see how you didn't take care of that bit and it's all slopped over the side of the pan; well, that'll burn when it's cooking and it'll ruin your pizza. Let's get rid of it, shall we? Then it'll be good."

She wipes a kitchen towel around the edge of Ollie's pizza tray so that his won't be ruined, and carries on her inspection of our lives.

"There's just one more thing to say, just one, and then you can cook your dinner. Did you see how I helped Ollie clean up the mess he'd made when he sloshed tomato paste over the side of the dough and onto the pizza tray? If I hadn't it wouldn't have been as good as it could have been. That's the same as being here in Beach Haven and having us adults here to help you clean up the mess that's been made in your lives so far. No one's saying that you have made the mess, but there's a mess there anyway, and you all need help to have it cleaned up so that you can carry on with your life and have it be the very best it can be. Do you all understand? That's what you're here for, and that's why we're here, to help you make really good choices that will make your life yummy and wonderful."

She smiles at us, and says, "Go on, go and cook them, and mind your fingers, don't get them burned!"

I take mine to one of the ovens and place it inside, then I go and sit with Ollie and Liam while we wait as the tantalizing smell fills the room and makes my appetite come back.

Miss Cassie continues to talk to us as we eat.

"So, think of your life as a pizza; whether your life is satisfying or nourishing will depend upon the amount of effort you put into making your pizza, your life."

My mouth is full of pizza.

"You get to choose what you put on your pizza, what will be satisfying to you, what you choose to have in your life. You choose. You can keep the people who have hurt you in your life (they're the sour pickles that are past their sell-by date) or you can choose the people that make you feel good. But *you* choose."

I'm listening to her as I eat. If I choose, then I choose that *he* is not on my pizza, or in my life, but how can I have a say on whether he's in my life or not? It's one thing choosing what's on a pizza, but I'm just a kid; how can I choose who's in my life? I swallow hard and speak out.

"I choose not to have my stepfather in my life; he's an anchovy and I don't like them, and I hate him."

Some kids laugh but it's not really funny, I'm not trying to be smart-mouthed.

"I can't stop him from being in my life, on my pizza...but he's poisoning my pizza and making me sick."

The kids are quiet, waiting to see what Miss Cassie will say. She's quiet for a moment.

"That's a tough one, isn't it? It *is* a bit like being forced to have anchovies on your pizza and being forced to eat them. I guess the whole point of this exercise is to acknowledge that *you* have the choice over how your pizza turns out. If you're forced to include anchovies, the way you deal with that is what will determine whether your pizza turns out to be okay or whether it's messed up. You could smash it to pieces or throw it away, or you could sit there and have a tantrum demanding that the anchovies are picked off, but you *could* gently pick them off and push them to the side of the plate and ignore them. It's the same as being forced to accept a new stepdad that you don't like. If you kick off and have a major tantrum you're just as likely to be told to "sit there until you eat it," and become trapped in a confrontation where no one wins. But if you accept that he's on your plate, you may find that you aren't forced to swallow it."

My appetite's gone again and I put down my fork.

I will never accept *him*, yet as I think about everything Miss Cassie's said while I lie in my bed, I wonder what would happen if I ignored him and just pushed him to the side of my plate. Would my pizza really be ruined just because it had anchovies on it, or could I still enjoy it even if I had to scrape them off and push them to the side of my plate? Can my life still be good even if *he's* in it? But as I think these thoughts I feel weighed down, for although it sounds good, I know *him* and I don't believe that he could ever settle for being shoved to the side of anyone's plate, let alone be scraped off into the trash. Why is it that my mom can't see what he's like, why did she have to go and marry him? We were happy before he came along.

Next morning we're in the Group Room and Miss Tina smiles at us.

"Miss Cassie tells me that you all made pizza last night and that you compared it to your lives. I like that idea, especially the idea that you are in charge of what you do in your lives and whether you make them good or bad, but there's one thing that I really want to make clear. All of you are here because the things that have happened to you in your lives so far have caused you pain, and it's important to know that although you are in charge of what you do with the rest of your lives, you are not responsible for all the bad things that have happened to you. That doesn't mean, though, that each of you didn't respond in a negative way that eventually led you to being here; we each have free will as to how we respond to the bad things that happen to us. Suicide can never be the right thing to do, ever, you're all too precious to be lost in such an act."

Several kids glance at each other and their discomfort tells me that that's why they're here.

"Right, let's get back to the pizza analogy. Do you all know what the word analogy means? It means to liken one thing to another, and that is useful to help explain something difficult. Analogies make pictures come into your head and that helps to make difficult things easier to understand. So, Miss Cassie used the analogy that your lives are like a pizza and you are in control of how they turn out.

"Let's think about the pride you felt when you'd finished making them. Did you feel pride?"

Most of the kids say "yes."

"What happens if you don't feel pride in your pizza, if you've messed it up and it doesn't taste good or nourish you? You still need to eat; everyone needs to eat to gain sustenance to survive. Will you try and eat from someone else's pizza? How many of you have heard of the term 'co-dependence'?"

"I have," Josie says. "My mom says that her sister and her husband are co-dependent...they're a mess, everything's always a drama. They're always splitting up and making up again. Is that what you mean?"

Miss Tina smiles and walks towards the flip chart, turning the page. She draws a three-piece jigsaw.

"This represents a whole person," she says, "Mr. John Doe," and then she draws another next to it. "And this represents Mrs. Jane Doe. Now, instead of these two people being separate and whole in their own right, they each behave as an incomplete person."

She erases two jigsaw pieces from Mr. John Doe and one from Mrs. Jane Doe and I get it; if a person is made up of three jigsaw pieces, then even though they're not whole people in their own right they can appear to be one person by fitting their pieces together.

"Co-dependence means that you don't feel whole as a person in your own right and need to have someone, anyone, in your life to make you feel whole." She points to the pieces of the jigsaw on the flip chart. "See how the pieces of an incomplete person fit to make what appears to be a whole person, but neither person is whole in their own right? They've lost part of themselves in the need to *fit* into the other person's jigsaw."

I stare at her drawing, my mind racing. Does my mom need *him* to fit with her jigsaw pieces? Somehow something dawns on me, something raw and something that makes me want to cry. Is it *him* that needs her to make him whole? Is he trying to take a part of her, the part that belongs to me and my mom, to make him whole?

Miss Tina carries on talking; my head is spinning.

"Everyone wants to have a partner in life, it's natural. Human beings are social creatures and aren't meant to be alone, but it's not okay to be in a relationship with someone who needs you to make them feel whole. This is where I really like the pizza analogy. Remember, Miss Cassie told you that your pizza was your life. Think about how it would feel to stand there admiring your pizza and the care you took to make it as good as it is, when someone that you like stands next to you. You see what a fine pizza they've made and you both want to share each other's pizzas. That's fine, that's how healthy relationships are made."

I remember last night when I shared my pizza with some of the kids and they shared theirs with me; it felt good.

"But imagine how it would feel if you stood there admiring your beautiful pizza when someone stands next to you whose pizza is a mess and not at all nourishing, and who hasn't taken any care with it. To feel full, or whole, that person will want to eat your pizza because his won't sustain him, but sharing with that person will not make *you* feel nourished, and eventually you won't feel full or satisfied; he will, but you won't."

The room's quiet. I wonder whether my mom thought *his* pizza was good and satisfying. I know she would have when she first met him because he tried really hard to make her believe that he was cool and that his life was together. But that was then. Since they got married she must be able to see that he's not at all together; he's a mess.

"Now, think about how it would feel if two people who were looking at each other's pizzas both had a messed up one that neither had taken any care over. Both will be hungry, knowing that their own pizza isn't going to nourish them or fill them up, so they grab at each other's pizzas, desperate to feel full or whole, but it can never happen because neither has enough for the other. That's co-dependence, and it's a very bad type of relationship to get into. It happens when people are desperate to be in a relationship, any relationship, and anyone will do, just so that they're not alone."

Is my mom like that? Was she desperate to be in a relationship, any relationship? But try as I might, I can't see her that way, for we were really happy on our own, and she'd never bothered to date before. So my thoughts drift off to the conclusion that *he* must be like that, seeking someone who has a good and nourishing pizza for him to feed off because his own is messed up. Suddenly it all makes sense to me and although I hate how awful and huge it seems, knowing that I can't do anything about it makes me feel calmer inside. I think I understand what's going on between my mom and *him*.

Josie says, "My aunt and uncle fight all the time. He accuses her of having an affair, and she accuses him as well. My mom says they're both having affairs."

Miss Tina frowns. "That's one of the problems with people in co-dependent relationships, neither feel as if they're getting enough from the other person. They never feel full, they feel empty most of the time so they go in search of someone else's pizza as well, to try and make themselves feel full, or whole, but they can never feel full in that type of relationship."

"Then how can they fix it?" Josie asks.

"They have to make their pizza better, more edible and more nutritious, and by that I mean that they have to work on themselves to make themselves feel whole as human beings. Then, and only then, will they be able to stand there whole and ready to be in a real relationship with someone who is equally as whole," she grins at us, "with a tasty, edible and nutritious pizza to offer."

All this talk of pizza is making me hungry.

"Let your pizza be as good as it can be and share it with respect; don't mess your own up so much that you have to seek someone and force them to share theirs because you can't survive with your own. Don't mess up yours so much that you need theirs to make you feel whole and nurtured. Make your life as good as it can be. Make good choices as to who and what you have in it, it's yours for the whole of your lifetime and you have to live with it. Choose people and things that will satisfy and nurture you to make you and your life as full as it can be."

My stomach's rumbling.

"Take care of your pizza, your life, and take pride in it. Choose what you want on it, make it how you want it to be, take control of it, and only share parts of yourself with those who value their own pizza, their life, in the same way you value yours. If you do these things, then you can share equally with someone and not become co-dependent."

"How do you know if your parents are co- what?" a kid asks.

"Co-dependent," Miss Tina says.

I blurt out. "Yeah, how do you know?"

Miss Tina looks at me hard and ignores the other kid, and I suddenly feel naked having spoken out.

"D'you think that your parents may be co-dependent, Shane?"

My face is red and the bruises on my face start smarting.

"Um, I don't know," I say, feeling embarrassed and wishing I'd kept my mouth shut.

"If life is like a pizza, does your mom take pride in hers?"

I'm quiet for a moment as I try to think. It's hard with all the kids staring at me and with thoughts of my mom hurting so much.

"I think so, well, she always seemed to, but not since she met *him*."

"You never say his name," Alison blurts out.

I'm instantly angry with her for forcing me to think of his name, but as soon as his name pops into my head I chase it away. I ignore her.

Silence settles over the Group Room as the kids look around waiting for what's going to happen next. Miss Tina speaks.

"Well, Shane, aren't you going to answer Alison? You do refer to your stepfather as '*he*' or '*him*.' Do you want to say why?"

I can feel my teeth clenched tightly together in anger and all of a sudden I can feel Anger Beads swelling all over me filled with hatred towards *him* and anger towards Alison. I hate it but I don't know how to make it go away, so I sit there sweating and fuming at the same time.

"Shane, this is a safe place, this is a place where we explore our feelings," Miss Tina says gently.

I have nowhere else to go but to answer her.

"I don't mention his name because all the time that I don't, then he doesn't exist to me..." my voice trails off, "...and I wish he didn't."

"That's a terrible thing to say," some kid says, and I feel as if my Anger Beads are about to burst and leave Anger Slime all over me; what does he know?

Something is in the room, something unspoken, as Miss Tina glances at the kid and he looks at the floor. I'm grateful to her, and suddenly I feel safe with her here. An image flashes into my head of my first night here when I lost control of myself and sobbed into her arms, wearing rabbit pajamas.

"He must have hurt you a lot for you to feel that way," Miss Tina says, and I wish she hadn't because the moment she says it something happens inside me, something I can't stop. I can hide the pain I feel at what that man's done to me, hide it behind anger, but I can't seem to control the pain I feel at what he's done to my mom. It's as raw as an open wound.

Everything happens so fast. I'm angry. I can't think straight and my heart is pounding. I'm sweating with Anger Beads that have already burst, leaving Anger Slime all over me, and then I lose it and start sobbing, as thoughts of my mom being hurt cascade over me, leaving me drowning in desperation.

Chapter Seven

The hollow silence in the Group Room is terrible, almost as bad as the emptiness in my heart. How can this have happened? I don't want to think about all of this...it's so much easier being angry than having to face what's going on inside you, what makes you who you are.

I'm embarrassed as the sound of my sobbing ebbs away, surrounded by silence that is punctuated by awkward coughs.

Miss Tina hands me a tissue and I wish it were as big as a sheet so that I could hide behind it.

It seems forever before I can slow my breathing and still my mind but it finally happens, and someone speaks very quietly and gently. It's almost as if her voice might break the fragile space between each of us but which surrounds all of us—it's a space filled with pain.

"I hate my stepfather, too; he raped me," Josie says. "I wish my mom never married him and I wish that he were dead, but wishing it doesn't make anything go away or get better. I wish it did."

She drifts off into a place where none of us can follow and instantly I feel ashamed of myself for focusing upon my own pain and anger when others in the group obviously have experienced as much, if not more, pain than I have. I don't know what to do; there's a plea on my lips but Miss Tina rescues me and I'm so grateful.

"Having a stepparent is difficult. It's difficult for everyone."

She stands up again.

"Let's explore what it means to have a stepparent and to be a stepparent, and also what it feel like to be your biological parent, the one that's often stuck in the middle."

She puts three chairs in the middle of the room and places a piece of paper in front of each chair that says, "child," "bio-parents" and "stepparents."

"Okay, who wants to go first?"

Josie raises her hand and I admire her. She smiles at me.

"Okay, sit in the 'child' seat and say how it feels to be a child in this family. Can you do that?"

She nods and I feel admiration for her. She glances at me as she settles into the seat.

"It feels very bad in this seat. I feel weighed down,

as if I'm going to drown under the weight of my parents arguing with each other, and their new partners feeding into it."

I'm listening.

Miss Tina says, "Okay, Josie, sit in the chair that represents your parents and say how it feels to be one of the parents in this family."

"My mom or my dad?"

"Either, but start with your dad."

Her voice suddenly becomes different and her voice is distorted with pain.

"I feel so guilty. If I hadn't left, then maybe that creep wouldn't have hurt my daughter. I don't know how to make it up to her."

"Now say how it feels to be your mom."

Josie's face suddenly looks angry. She cusses violently. "It's all your fault. If you hadn't left, then none of this would have happened." Then her voice changes and becomes whiny. "How was I to know he was a pervert and was going to hurt my kids?"

Miss Tina smiles at Josie and something churns in my stomach as I feel admiration for her sitting in the middle of the room being so honest in front of us all. I glance around the room and see Alison look away quickly, and suddenly she doesn't look so good to me.

"Are you okay, Josie?" When she nods Miss Tina asks her to sit in the other chair and tell us how it feels to be a stepparent.

A flash of fear shoots across Josie's face.

"I can't be *him*."

My face flickers with a smile as she calls her step-father "*him*," yet the hairs on the back of my neck bristle as I hear the fear in her voice.

"Of course not," Miss Tina says, "but say how it feels to be your dad's new wife."

"Oh, okay," she sounds relieved, clears her throat and immediately sounds whiny.

"Why do you put up with it? What's wrong with you, are you scared of her, or what? Tell her, go on, tell her. Demand when you're going to see the kids, don't put up with it."

Miss Tina holds up her hand. "Okay, we get the picture, but tell us what it feels like for your dad's new wife to be in this family."

Josie looks at her quizzically for a moment and then her voice becomes lower; there's an edge to it that sounds as if she's about to cry.

"You still love your ex, don't you? I'm scared you're going to go back to her. Your kids hate me and resent me because they think I made you leave. It's not fair because I didn't make you leave, you did it on your own, yet I get the blame. I'm sick of being the bad guy in all of this. You should stand up and face the blame instead of letting it be dumped on me."

Silence fills the room. Josie looks shocked. We're all staring at her.

She bursts into tears and I swallow a lump in my throat. Nothing is as it seems until you start to wear someone else's shoes. This is *so* hard.

Miss Tina hands her a tissue and waits until she blows her nose before speaking.

"What have you learned?" she asks.

Josie sniffs and then says, "That there's more than one way of seeing things and that each person has a different take on things...and...maybe things aren't quite the way they first seem when you look a little deeper."

"Very good," Miss Tina says. "You learned that your father feels guilty and your mother feels angry, but you also learned that your stepmother feels caught, she's an outsider yet she's also part of your family, a very important part, too. It's hard on you because you didn't ask for her to come into your life, it was just thrust upon you, you had no say in it all, but you have to live with the consequences of your parents' actions."

Josie's nodding and as I look around I can see lots of kids nodding. I nod myself.

"It's doubly hard on you, though, because your mother's choice of new partner turned out to be a pedophile, which has had devastating consequences upon you, but it's also had a bad consequence on your parents. Both feel guilty, for different reasons, that their decisions, which you didn't ask for, have hurt you. It's hard," Miss Tina gives Josie a hug, "but you'll be all right."

She goes back to her chair and shoots me a look.

"Who'd like to go next?" Miss Tina asks, and suddenly everyone's quiet, deadly quiet. I shift in my seat and I'm just about to stare at the floor when Josie catches my eye again and there's something in her face, something that challenges me without words. I feel my stomach turn over and although I try desperately to find a spot on the floor to focus upon, I'm drawn towards her gaze as she continues to stare at me.

I feel as if I'm in a dream as I stand up and walk towards the three chairs in the middle of the room. Miss Tina is smiling at me and suddenly I feel really sheepish and silly, but that feeling doesn't last for long because as soon as I sit on the chair marked "child" I feel scared.

"Thank you, Shane," Miss Tina says. "So how does it feel being a kid in your family?"

I try to think but it's hard, my head keeps spinning and the hair on the back of my neck is bristling with fear. The kids are watching me and waiting for me to say something. I focus upon Miss Tina and try to ignore them. How *does* it feel to be a kid in my "family"? It feels like hell, so I say, "It feels like hell. I just want to get away. I hate '*him*' so much." I stare at Alison as I refuse to use his name, and she looks angry. "He's ruined everything between me and my mom, and I know he knows he's doing it."

"Doing what?" Miss Tina asks.

"Instigating me, picking on me, getting me into trouble and then laughing at me behind my mom's back so that she can't see. He does it all the time, and then I get into trouble when I react to him...like earlier."

I can feel Anger Beads on my skin threatening to burst all over me, covering me with Anger Slime, as I think about him.

"Okay, Shane, swap chairs and sit in the step-parent chair and say how it feels to be your stepfather."

I don't really want to—but everyone's eyes are on me, so to avoid losing face I swap chairs, and I can't believe how different I suddenly feel. It's weird—suddenly I seem to *be* him and it's almost as if I've gotten fatter and taller, and I swear that my voice sounds different as I speak.

"Ha ha, gotcha, you little creep. You think you're going to get all your mom's attention, no way, she's mine and I'm not sharing her with anyone, especially not some spotty faced kid like you. I'm bigger than you, cleverer, too. Shout as loud as you like but she'll believe me because I know how to make her believe me. You're just a stupid kid that kicks off, and when you do that you behave just as I want you to, and you damn yourself. Yeah!"

I can hear my voice sounding triumphant and it feels so weird to say what I know he thinks about me.

My Anger Beads have burst and I'm covered in vile Anger Slime, which leaves me no place to go other than to accept the things I've just said out loud.

"Sit in the parent's chair and tell us how it feels to be your mom," Miss Tina says, piercing my thoughts.

I swap chairs again and suddenly my stomach churns badly and I long to cry all over again. Damn it, what's happening to me?

Miss Tina's voice is gentle. "Shane, how does it feel to be your mother in this family?"

The lump in my throat threatens to stop me from breathing as images of her trying to hug me in the hall earlier but being held back by *him* flash in front of me.

I cough, trying to clear my throat of the pain that rests there.

"What's happening? Why has everything gone wrong? I just wanted us to be happy. Why are you both behaving this way?"

My hands are trembling as I voice what I think my mom would say, and as my mouth makes the sounds my heart aches for my mom and the closeness we once shared, feelings I've buried so deeply. Miss Tina puts her hand on my shoulder and feeling its weight brings me back into the room and stops my head from spinning so badly. I look around and the kids are staring at me, some are smiling...Josie's smiling.

"So, by stepping into your mom's shoes you can

see that she feels confused and a bit lost. D'you think that it's fair to say that she married your stepfather in good faith with the hopes that you could all live together happily? Do you?" she asks me.

I hate it but I have to agree with her. Yes, I guess she did think that we would be a happy little family. I didn't ask for it though; I was happy when it was just us, but she obviously wanted something else and thought that having him around would make me happy, too. It seems crazy but likely.

"D'you think that she hoped he'd be a father figure to you?" she asks.

I find it difficult not to spit out my words. I'd rather die than have him as my father.

"Put yourself in your mother's shoes, Shane. Do you think your mom thought that by marrying him, he would be able to provide some of the things she wasn't able to give you as a woman and a mother?"

I'm immediately irritated because Miss Tina's words remind me of the day Mom had first told me that she was getting married. She'd said, "Just think, he'll be able to do guy-stuff with you. You can go fishing and play baseball." Didn't she know that I didn't want to do those things, and if I ever wanted to I could do them with my friend's dad? She didn't need to marry someone in order to provide those things for me, and hell, he hasn't done any guy-stuff with me since he moved in. He's not interested in me; all he cares about is getting me out of the way.

"D'you think that your mom might have thought it would be good for a teenage boy to have a man around?" Miss Tina asks again.

I nod slowly. "I guess."

"Okay, so if that was one of your mom's reasons for getting married, then how do you think she's feeling now, since those things haven't happened and your relationship with your stepfather has deteriorated so badly?"

I shrug. "Bad, I guess."

"What else will she be feeling?"

I look at Miss Tina with a frown on my face.

"Come on, Shane, you know your mother, what else will she be feeling?"

My head's spinning again and my voice becomes a whisper.

"She'll be scared and devastated, and she won't know what to do."

Tears prick my eyes again as I realize that it's not only me that feels betrayed and hurt...she does, too. But then it dawns on me, as I remember the look of pain on her face when she tried to pull away from *him* earlier today: she'll be feeling controlled and powerless. That's how I feel around him.

"And is that how you feel?" Miss Tina asks.

I nod. I want to cry but I've got nothing left inside me. I feel dry and barren.

"I just want him to go away," I say, feeling empty and helpless, my Anger Slime slipping towards the floor, settling in my socks. I'd have smiled at the image had I been thinking about anything other than the pain and helplessness I feel, and that I'm sure my mom feels, too.

I stand up and walk back to my chair, my heart heavy.

Ollie asks a question and we all look at him.

"Yeah, but what happens if Shane's got it all wrong? I mean, I hated my stepdad when he first moved in and I sounded just like Shane. I was really angry and everything he did was wrong, no matter how much he tried to fit in, but after a while when I realized that he was staying and that nothing I did to upset him would make him go away, I saw him differently. He was okay. It was just me not wanting to share my mom with anyone else. How can you be sure that Shane isn't just going through that?"

"Good question, Ollie, and it's a tough one to answer. It's normal for the kids in a family to take time to adjust to a stepparent. Remember, they didn't ask for their parents to get a divorce nor did they ask to have two new parents to deal with, but it's something that they have to cope with, and it takes time for everything to settle down. Everyone in this *new* family suddenly has a different role to play...they have to learn how to say goodbye to their old role and learn how to feel comfortable with their new role. It doesn't matter how prepared you think you are for it, it still takes time and is a huge adjustment, and if that's how it is for stable caring parents, then how is it for parents who aren't so stable?"

I've always thought that my mom was stable; she's had Grandpa to tell her what to do and how to be.

"Now, I want you to think back to Miss Cassie's lesson about life being like a pizza and the work we did on co-dependence."

We're all looking at her as she carries on.

"What happens when one of your parents remarries someone whose pizza is messed up, who sees you and your mother sharing each other's pizza happily, each giving the same back in return and each feeling nurtured and full? What is the new stepparent going to feel when he or she looks at their own inadequate pizza?"

Suddenly it all becomes clearer to me when I imagine *him* standing there with a messed up pizza that will leave him starving hungry, watching me and Mom sharing our tasty, satisfying pizzas with each other. He's going to feel really jealous, empty and hungry. He'll see me as a threat, because if I eat from my mom's pizza then there'll be less for him, and he can't allow that to happen, so in order to satisfy himself he has to get rid of me.

I don't want to think these things because they're painful, but even as the thoughts fire through me uncontrollably, despite the raw pain, suddenly I can see, really *see*. It hurts even more when I think about the pizza analogy, for if I'm standing there with my well-made pizza, offering to share it with others, okay, with *him* too, then why can't he share in my pizza, get to know me and enjoy my pizza? Why does he feel the need to get rid of it or smash it so that neither he nor Mom can enjoy it? As I think these blinding thoughts that leave me nowhere to hide, I realize that if he messes up my pizza, he hopes that she'll share his, now that she can't share mine.

"So, what's your stepfather going to feel when he looks at his own inadequate pizza when he can see you and your mom enjoying each others'?" Miss Tina asks again.

"He's going to panic that he's not going to get enough to be able to survive, and so he'll get rid of anyone that gets in the way of him feeding off the pizza he wants."

"Exactly," Miss Tina says, "Well put."

"That's sick," is all I can think of to say.

My head is still spinning and I'm only vaguely aware that Josie is smiling at me across the Group Room.

Ollie speaks out again. "Yeah, but," he says, with a frown on his face, "what happens if your new step-parent's pizza is a good one yet you're so angry with your mom or dad for finding someone else that you deliberately try to mess up your own pizza so that you don't have to share yours with them? What happens if you deliberately try to make trouble in order to drive off the new partner and split them up?"

"It's a hard call," Miss Tina says, "and I guess only you can know the answer to that. If you find your relationship messed up with your stepparent, or your parents for that matter, you have to ask yourself the question, 'What did *I* do?' If you can truthfully say that you did nothing that would cause trouble between your parent and your new stepparent and your life is suddenly messed up, if your pizza is suddenly messed up and no longer satisfying, then it can be attributed to someone else. But only if you can truthfully say that you did nothing to cause any trouble."

She looks at me.

"Shane, look inside your heart and answer the question, 'Did you deliberately mess up your pizza so that no one could share it, or do you think that someone else tried to mess things up so badly that you wouldn't be able to share your pizza with your mother, and then she wouldn't be able to share yours?"

I can't answer. I look around me in this room where everyone is painfully honest and I can't stop myself from thinking thoughts that flash into my mind. Did I ever try to get along with *him*, did I? No, if I'm honest, I didn't. I just wanted him to go away because I wanted my mom for myself; we've always been so happy, or so I thought. Yet something clouds my thinking. I'm prepared to accept responsibility for behaving badly around him at times and I can be honest and admit that I didn't want Mom to marry him, but I can't accept responsibility for the way he behaves around me.

I sit up straight feeling suddenly animated. Yes, I can own my part in this mess. I didn't want him to marry my mom; I didn't want him to move into our house...we didn't need him. I'm nearly a man. I can take care of things around the house. Granddad showed me how. But, you know, even after accepting that I put up brick walls to keep him out because I didn't like him, something still feels wrong. Aren't adults supposed to know more than kids? Aren't they supposed to take more responsibility and try to make things as good as they can be? If he were for real, wouldn't he try his hardest to get to know me, to try and break down the brick wall I've built around myself? Wouldn't he offer his pizza to me and want to share mine? He hasn't done any of those things.

I shut my eyes knowing that everyone is staring at me waiting for an answer, and I force my brain to actually see all three of us standing in a line each holding a pizza. The answer is inside me, I know it is, I just have to look and see.

I can see Mom smiling at me holding her pizza out, wanting to share it with me—well, not just me, everyone; my mom's kind and gives to everyone. I see myself holding my own pizza and I'm not very pleased with what I see...I'm backing away, looking scared and unsure. I don't look as if I'm willing to share my pizza, but then when I force my mind to see *him* I understand why I'm backing away. There's something nasty in his face and he's got something in his hand but it doesn't look like any pizza I've seen before, and it certainly isn't anything like Mom's or mine. He's staring at Mom's pizza and then at mine, and then I realize what it is that I see in his face— it's jealousy—and that's when I pull away and don't want to share my pizza with him. I don't want any of his pizza, if that's what it is...it's a mess, and I don't want him to be anywhere near mine. He feels unsafe and deep down I feel scared.

I open my eyes, dumbfounded that I can find the answer to Miss Tina's questions and my own searchings just by looking within myself. I sit up straight and suddenly feel more confident. I feel that I've been really honest with myself, and that gives me the confidence I need to be able to speak out and own my feelings and attitudes in front of these kids.

"I don't believe that I deliberately messed up my own pizza so that I didn't have to share it with anyone...I want to share it with my mom, my Granddad and all my family and friends...I want to share with other people, but there's something wrong with *him*, something that winds me up, but also scares me. Something's not right, I just know it. I don't have the right words for it, but I know that something's not right with him."

Miss Tina smiles at me, and says, "Shane, everyone has to trust their intuition, that small voice inside you that knows the truth. Trust your gut feelings, your gut instinct, for it's almost always right. But you also need to ask yourself the question, 'What did *I* do?' so that you get a clearer picture of what's really going on."

"I did," I say quickly. "I searched inside myself to see what I had done that might have made things worse, and I have to admit that I did do things that made it worse. I was hurt that my mom wanted someone else when we were so close."

I hang my head and look at the floor.

"I was jealous of them being together. I felt left out, so I did things that I felt would make them pay."

"That's normal," Miss Tina says, enabling me to look up again.

"I shut him out. I just wanted him to go away. I just wanted things to go back to being normal."

"That's normal, too," Miss Tina says, with a sad look upon her face. "It takes a while for everyone to adjust to someone new coming into the family and each having a different role to play. It's even harder when there are stepbrothers and sisters because they all need to establish a place in the new 'blended' family. It's not easy, but the grown-ups are the ones that need to help the kids to make it happen...it's not the kids that need to make it happen for the adults."

I can feel my face twisting with pain.

"Mom tried her hardest," my voice breaks, "but he never did anything to help make it right. I really believe that he didn't care, he just wanted me out of the way so that he could have Mom all for himself."

I'm talking too fast and I glance around the room, suddenly desperate for the kids to hear me and to understand that I'm not being a brat but that something is seriously wrong with my stepfather. There, I admitted that he is my stepfather.

I can see some kids nodding, some smiling, others frowning, trying to make sense of it all, how sharing pizzas is the same as sharing yourself, and I see Alison glaring at me but Josie is smiling. It's not the usual boy-girl smile that gives you permission to tread a little closer, it's a "high-five good job" smile and it makes me feel warm all over; it's a smile that encourages me to speak out again.

"It happened little by little. The more he tried to push me away and get me into trouble with my mom, the more I didn't want to have anything to do with him; but then I guess, the more distant I became, the more he picked on me. No, what am I saying? That's not right. It doesn't feel right. I believe that he wanted me to be distant, he wanted me out of the way so that he could have my mom all to himself—he didn't want to share his pizza or share mine. He wanted me out of the way and my mom all for himself. I really believe that."

I sigh and realize that I've been talking really fast

as if my courage may fail me if I take my time to say what's in my mind and heart.

Miss Tina looks at me and the room is still with everyone waiting to hear what she has to say. I listen too. Is she going to tell me I'm crazy, a jealous spoiled kid who has a crazy close relationship with his mom, or is she going to hear me, I mean *really* hear me? I can hear the clock ticking loudly in the Group Room, as we're all quiet. She looks at me and then around the room.

"Do you know what it feels like to be disbelieved? Do you?"

Almost all the kids murmur, "Yes," and so do I.

"One of the most important things we do here at Beach Haven is to help you all learn how to be objective...that means to weigh up the 'rights' and the 'wrongs' of every given situation so that you can make an informed choice...you can work things out for yourself and be fairly sure that you've got it right. One of the ways to do that is to get into someone else's shoes so that you understand their take on things, how it feels from their perspective, and then also to seriously question yourself and your behavior. That's why we always ask the question, 'What did *you* do?' If you can own your behavior and accept how much or how little you contributed to a situation and still find that you don't have the answer, then you can look elsewhere for the answer and ask the question, 'What did *they* do? Does that make sense?"

I nod. Yes, it makes sense. I now know what part I played in our relationship. I wasn't perfect, in fact I was a jerk, but my behavior still doesn't answer my questions, so I have to look towards his behavior to find the answers and I don't like what I see.

I hold up my hand, my fear of speaking drowned out by my need to clarify myself in front of all these kids who saw me kick-off earlier today. They must think I'm a prize jerk. No one here uses aggression to express themselves, they don't fight or argue, nor do they think it's big to fight or wear bruises like trophies to show how hard you are. The currency here in Beach Haven appears to be honesty, and it costs a lot. As my bruises from juvenile still smart I should feel broke, yet I don't, I feel rich. Today has been a long day; I've paid with pain for the honesty I've found within myself, and for the honesty I've been given here within the Group Room.

I'm tingling as we leave the room.

Chapter Eight

My head is still spinning when I get into bed, although part of me feels better because I can understand what's going on inside of me and that makes me feel free. Understanding is everything... where did I hear those words, "There's no blame, only understanding"? I don't know.

I lie there listening to the sounds of the ocean crashing up the shore outside, and the sounds let me know that I'm alive and safe. There's an emptiness that threatens to swamp me as thoughts of my mom flow through me. I want to be with her but right now it's just too painful to think about her. Yet as I try to block her out of my thoughts, she seeps back into my mind. I wonder if she's thinking about me and if she's safe. It turns my stomach to think of her being unsafe...I don't know what to do to help her...and as my helplessness overwhelms me I wonder if she's lying in her bed feeling as helpless as I feel. Is she wondering whether I'm safe? Is she missing me? I struggle with my feelings, for I long for her to miss me and to come to Beach Haven and claim me, so that we could live as we used to before *he* intruded into our lives, but I know that it'll never happen. Why is it so hard to be a teenager? I don't understand. Why should it be so hard to love your parent and yet feel such anger and betrayal when they invite someone new into their lives and disregard your feelings? Where's my dad? Why did he have to go away and leave me to deal with all of this?

I hear the waves crashing on the shore, riding up the sand, its foamy froth spreading a line on the sand. I listen and listen ...and suddenly it's tomorrow and I wake up with the sun in my eyes.

I stand under my shower and it's hot and wonderful. I visualize my body covered in Anger Slime and I scrub and scrub making myself clean and free from all the mess that threatens to drag me down with it, to be drowned by hatred and anger. No, I'm not going to let that happen; I'm going to fight my feelings and I'm going to get rid of all my anger. I'm going to scrub myself spotless until my anger and hatred are washed away with the soapsuds, down the drain.

My resolution doesn't last, though, because right after breakfast I'm called to a family session and there *he* is, sitting in an armchair smirking at me when Mom's not looking at him. I can feel my heart beginning to race, heat flashing through me, and as I start to sweat I imagine hundreds of Anger Beads glistening on my skin. I don't know what to do. I sit on the edge of my chair, my fists clenched, trying to control myself.

Miss Tina seems to sense what's happening inside me and breaks the ice by talking.

"You should be very proud of Shane, he's been working very hard since he got here."

"I am," Mom says, shooting me a bleak smile but I barely hear her because all I hear is *him* laughing under his breath.

An Anger Bead has just burst around my neck and it itches really badly.

Miss Tina turns to face him and says, "Sir, part of the work that Shane's done is to try and understand other people's point of view, how it feels to be that person and what they're thinking. It means enacting that person by copying the way they communicate with other people, saying what they would say and exploring what their non-verbal communication is saying. We may *say* one thing but what we really feel shows in our body language. Your body language, sir, shows a total lack of respect and concern for Shane..." she pauses and then smiles sweetly at him, "and I wonder if you're aware of it? You know, sometimes we give out the wrong message through careless gestures or facial expressions. I'm sure you're very proud of Shane, too."

Mom looks terrified but I feel great, for Miss Tina has just stood up to him. He looks furious but he's got nowhere to go because she's cornered him. He either has to lie and agree that he's proud of me, or else admit that he hates me and that he shows it in his body language. I hold my breath waiting to see which way he's going to play it.

He takes his sweater off and it occurs to me that he's got Anger Beads threatening to burst over his skin too, and I know I'm right because he starts scratching at his neck, which is rapidly turning red.

"It's a shame he doesn't do right at home then," he says defensively.

I look at Miss Tina wondering what she's going to say, and I feel as if I'm watching a game of volleyball, with my honor being the ball.

"I'm afraid you didn't answer my question, sir. Are you aware that your non-verbal communication shows a total lack of respect or concern for your stepson?"

I wince inside when she calls me that; I don't want to be his "anything," but as I will myself to stay in control, I realize that she's trying to force him to accept that we have a relationship, even though neither of us wants it. I remember her saying that stepparents are the adults, and even if it's difficult to adjust at first, adults should make the effort...it shouldn't be the kids that have to make it right for them.

"What is this?" he starts to shout. "I didn't come here for this. How dare you speak to me like that? Come on, we're going," he says standing up, and starts to pull at Mom's arm.

Miss Tina stands.

"Sit down, please, sir. This is a place where we speak honestly, where we hear things that are difficult and where we deal with them. This is what Shane has been doing...and as you can see it's not always comfortable."

He sits back down, again having nowhere to go, for if he walks out, then he's not as brave as I am because he couldn't deal with hearing things he didn't want to hear, whereas I could. I know he'll never let me look better than him, so he sits back down, and Mom breathes out.

My Anger Beads seem to have gone and I feel calmer. Miss Tina is in charge and I feel safe as she starts to talk.

"Coming into a family that's already established can be hard," she says, looking at him but he stares at the floor, sulking. "Are you finding it hard, sir?"

"Hell, no. He's a spoiled brat, a momma's boy. He's done everything he can to run me off but it ain't gonna happen." I can feel my Anger Beads brewing again on my forehead as my stomach churns. He looks my way and snarls at me. "She's mine now, not yours. She's my *wife*; you need to get that into your thick head."

Miss Tina shoots me a warning glance, one that reminds me of a referee in a boxing ring trying to hold one man away from the one that's on the floor, and I realize that I'm the one on the floor. I'm just a kid, I don't have any power at all and he's a bully, someone who has to win even against someone younger or smaller. He's someone who doesn't care about anything except getting what he wants, and what he wants is my mom all for himself. He wants me out of the way and he'll do whatever he has to do to make that happen. I feel like I'm on the boxing ring floor counting up to ten while he's waiting to pounce on me and hit me again with everything he's got.

Mom's crying and seeing her upset crucifies me, so although my Anger Beads are bursting all over me and I want to kill him, now that his hatred of me is out in the open, suddenly he doesn't matter, the only thing that matters to me is my mom. I reach for a box of tissues and stand to give them to Mom.

Miss Tina's right about non-verbal communication, showing what you really think and feel without using any words, because as I hand the box to Mom, no one says anything yet everything in the room is shouting at me. Mom looks at me with something on her face that says, "I love you so much...I never really left you," and Miss Tina, although gripping the side of her armchair when I stood up so quickly, has trust on her face, but what's written on his face shrieks the loudest. He hates me, there's no doubt, it's there on his face, and he doesn't even have the brains to try and hide it. Suddenly everything he feels is laid bare for us all to see, and it's not very pretty.

This is a place of honesty, Miss Tina keeps telling me, and nothing could be more honest than what's in this room right this minute.

He looks at me and I can feel the hatred coming off him.

"Look at you," he says, his voice hissing like a venomous snake. "It's sick. Momma's boy, momma's boy, momma's crying, let me get you a tissue," he whines, his face full of disgust, as I leap out of my chair.

Mom's sobbing and my heart is broken. I don't know what to do, for my Anger Beads burst all over me, leaving me covered in anger and hatred. I'm torn between flying at his throat and between comforting my mom, but Miss Tina's voice steps in to take away my indecision and I'm so grateful, for at this moment my anger is such that I could kill him and spend the rest of my life in jail. It's a moment where I'm teetering on the edge of a precipice, my toes poking over, my balance gone, yet Miss Tina grabs me before I fall into a place from which I can't return. My heart is hammering. My Anger Slime covers every part of my body; my nostrils are flaring with hatred as I see him laughing while my mom sobs. It's as if my life hangs in the balance. I want to kill him; it rages through me and I'm suffocated by my hatred. It is this moment that will decide what happens to me in my life. I can attack his sneering face and try to snuff out his life, which is what I want to do if I'm honest with myself, but I can say goodbye to my life because I know that I'll spend years in prison being some big-guy's girl.

Miss Tina stands and steps towards me. Something in her eyes holds me—she knows what I'm feeling, she knows how angry I am and she knows the truth. I can see in her face that she believes everything I told her about how life was in my house. She can see my mom in pieces and she can see what a bully *he* is, and then I realize that if she can see these things, then she can see my pain.

"Sir, that's enough. Please stop it. I cannot allow you to be abusive to a child in my care. Ma'am, if you allow him to abuse you then I can't stop him, but I can stop him being abusive to any child that's a resident of Beach Haven."

It's hard to say what I'm feeling because my mom's just shown me that she's been there for me all the time but I just haven't been able to see it. I thought she didn't want me anymore because she had him, but now I can see that she's in as much pain as I am. She's crying uncontrollably and he's standing, jabbing his finger at Miss Tina, and although he's loads taller that she is, she stands tall in front of him, holding her head high, with her chin jutting forward.

"You will *not* be abusive to any child at Beach Haven...sir," she adds to be respectful.

It amazes me because he sits down. Mom's a mess; she's crying and wringing her hands. I go back to my seat, but as I watch her I'm destroyed seeing her in pieces. We're sitting in our chairs staring at each other, not knowing where to go or how to extract ourselves from this mess. He becomes quiet, very quiet and I have a sense that he's met his match, that he feels beaten. But then a feeling seeps into me and I know that his surrender is only temporary, for when he doesn't have someone strong like Miss Tina around, he'll start pushing his weight around and bully us again.

"What can *you* do to make this family work?" she asks him, while Mom blots her nose and tries to control herself. My stomach is in shreds; I just can't cope when my mom is hurting. Y'know, some kids think it's weird to be so close to your mom, but I think they're wrong. I think that every kid has a right to be close to their parents, and what's between my mom and me is so special that anyone looking on would feel jealous. It dawns on me then that *he* is jealous and a part of me feels a bit sorry for him, but it's short lived when he answers Miss Tina.

He just shrugs and whines, "It's him, he ruins everything."

I look at him and suddenly everything is clear, and a calmness settles over me.

I say, "Your pizza's messed up."

He cusses at me badly and tells me to shut my mouth, but Mom looks at me with a frown on her face.

"What d'you mean?" she asks in a small voice.

"He's talking trash, trying to be smart-mouthed as usual."

"What d'you mean?" she asks again.

So I tell her all I've learned about being co-dependent, about needing someone else to make you feel whole and satisfied because your own pizza, or life, is messed up and you can't make it on your own as a whole person.

He's like a raging bull; his face is fuming and just by looking at him I know that his Anger Beads have burst and his Anger Slime is pulling him down, deep down, to a place where there's no way back. He hates me, it's there in his face for us all to see, there's no pretense anymore. I feel scared, wondering, *What will Mom do, now that she can see it?*

It's as if time stands still with each of us feeling shocked at the hatred in the room, and each waiting to see what the other will do. We don't have long to wait because he jumps up, grabs Mom by the arm, saying, "We're leaving, and you'll be hearing from my lawyer tomorrow," to Miss Tina.

But Mom snatches her arm away from him, and for the first time in my life I can see Anger Beads forming on her face. She never gets angry. I don't know who's more surprised, me or *him*.

"No, I'm not coming. I'm not doing this anymore. It's over. All this time I've believed you over Shane; you're so convincing. How could you? He's a kid and he's part of me."

He grabs her again and shouts, "You're coming with me."

Miss Tina and I jump up at the same time.

"Get off her," I scream, as all my feelings of love for my mom come flooding back, feelings that had never really gone but had just been hiding behind my sense of betrayal.

Miss Tina grabs my shirt to stop me from dumping all my anger on him, and she raises her voice.

"Sir, you need to leave right now."

He pushes Mom away and hisses into my face, cussing badly.

"You did this, you wrecked my marriage." Then he turns to Mom and says, "If you don't come now, it's over."

It seems crazy to me...didn't Mom just tell him that it was over? How can he turn around and give her an ultimatum?

She sounds calm. "It *is* over, as of now."

He cusses badly as he slams the door, and Mom and I look at each other, not really knowing what to do next.

Miss Tina asks us to sit.

"Well, where do we go from here?" she asks us.

I can't help it, I start crying. I'm so angry and my anger's got nowhere to go now that *he's* gone, so I cry instead. I feel stupid and mad at myself, but Mom comes over to me and holds me.

"I'm so sorry," she says in my ear. "Please forgive me. I had no idea. I'm *so* sorry."

Then she's crying and I try to comfort her.

"I'm sorry I put you through all this. I didn't know what else to do. I tried to tell you but you didn't believe me, so I figured that if I acted bad you'd have to listen to me. Then when I went to juvenile I was so angry and scared that I just lost it."

Then I'm crying again and she's trying to comfort me.

"Shane, I'm so sorry. I thought he was a good man, I really did. He seemed so sweet and kind. Remember when we went on that picnic by the river and he taught you how to fish? I just thought that having him around would be good for you. I'm your mom and I'll always love you no matter what, but I felt that you needed a man around to help you turn into a man. I don't know how to do that for you...I can do everything else, but I'm not a man."

Miss Tina speaks out as Mom sits back down.

"It's love that'll turn a boy into a man."

Mom looks terrible as she answers Miss Tina. "I didn't know what to do. He seemed so wonderful, but the moment we got married he changed. I mean, it was instant. I couldn't believe it. I was so afraid and I thought that if I could just make him feel important enough, then he'd be the same sweet guy I agreed to marry; but no matter how hard I tried, it just got worse. If I showed any affection to Shane he'd be so hateful towards him, so for his own safety I withdrew and gave him less attention."

She's crying really hard saying, "I'm sorry" over and over. Miss Tina smiles at me and when I go to stand up to comfort Mom again she puts her hand out and shakes her head, so I sit back down. I remember that at Beach Haven we face our feelings and the things we've done even if it's painful, but that doesn't stop my pain at seeing my mom in such a mess.

I sit there with my stomach in knots until she stops crying. Her face is all red and blotchy, and she blows her nose noisily, then looks at Miss Tina for guidance.

"We all do what we think is best at the time and in good faith. You said that your husband was 'convincing.' Say a little more."

Mom sniffs. "He *was* convincing. I see now that he was just acting at being a sweet, gentle person and that wasn't the real him at all."

"Some people can be very convincing, especially if there's something wrong with them."

"What d'you mean?" Mom asks.

"From what you describe and from the behavior I saw here today, it's likely that your husband has experienced problems in his childhood that have stopped him from developing into a well-balanced adult. Let's go back to the pizza analogy, since it's so helpful for explaining co-dependency. If your husband's pizza was so messed up due to bad things happening to him as a child, then he'd want to hide it, because if it were in such a mess, no one would want to share it with him and he'd be all alone. If he tried to tidy up the edges of his pizza and perhaps cover it with some extra cheese to hide the mess," she's grinning at us and I smile back as she makes pictures come into my head, "then for a short time he could present it as being whole and okay. Tell me, did he insist on getting married quickly?" Miss Tina asks Mom.

"Yes, he did." Mom looks confused. "How did you know?"

"It's very common. Think about it...if his pizza was so messed up and he was trying to hide his real self from you, then he could only keep up that pretense for a short time. If you had waited before getting married, he'd have shown his true self, because no one can maintain that amount of effort for very long."

"He insisted. He broke down and cried saying that it would mean everything to him if we could marry on the anniversary of his mother's death." She shakes her head. "How could I have been so gullible? I just thought that he was being really sensitive and sweet. I feel so stupid."

Miss Tina shakes her head. "Don't beat yourself up about it. You're not stupid at all. People that are so damaged have to be really convincing—their life depends upon it."

Mom frowns.

"Everyone needs love from other people; it's what keeps us whole and emotionally stable. If he had revealed the true state of his pizza to anyone, then no one would have wanted to be anywhere near him and he would have been loveless and alone. That would seem intolerable to him and he would defend against his true self being discovered at any cost, and unfortunately the cost was Shane."

"I feel so bad," Mom sniffs.

"Don't. You did what you thought was the best at the time. Your husband's pizza was so messed up that he needed yours to make him feel sustained, and his fear of being alone was so great that he couldn't tolerate seeing you share any of your pizza with Shane. He would have felt a real sense of not surviving...a subconscious sense that he would starve to death if he couldn't have *all* of you, so he had to discredit Shane in any way he could."

"How could I have been so stupid?" Mom says again, shaking her head.

"Like you said, he was very convincing and worked hard to get Shane into trouble without you seeing that he had instigated him."

"He did it all the time," I say. "It drove me crazy

because he'd sit behind you and laugh at me when you told me off, yet as soon as you turned around, he'd stop."

Mom shakes her head and mutters, "I'm sorry," over and over again.

"Can you see that the more he was able to get Shane into trouble and put distance between you both, the less you shared your pizza with Shane, and that meant 'more for him.'"

"It's sick," I say, but as Miss Tina talks and uses the pizza analogy to explain what's happened in our family, I understand and I can see that Mom does, too.

"It may be sick," Miss Tina says, "but that's how it is. Can you see why he behaved the way he did, Shane? Remember one of my favorite sayings, 'There's no blame, only understanding.' If you can understand why people behave the way they do, it reduces the blame you feel. Blame is such a negative feeling and it keeps your anger alive. I know it may seem hard right this minute to let go of the blame you feel, but in time as you come to understand everything, the blame you feel will go."

Right at this minute I don't believe her because I feel eaten up with blame, not towards my mom but towards *him*. She nods at me, reading the doubt in my face and I give her a bleak smile.

I can hear the other kids running up the hall and suddenly I want to leave, not that I'm mad at my mom anymore, I just want to get away from the heaviness and trauma that still seems to be hovering around the room. Miss Tina seems to sense my feelings and tells me to leave, so I hug my mom, who starts crying again. She tells me that she loves me and I tell her I love her, too.

Some kids are in the lounge and others are outside. I feel hemmed in as my thoughts race around my head, so I go outside and walk down to the beach. The sand scrunches beneath my feet.

"Hey, wait up," Josie calls, following me from the playground. We sit down on the warm sand.

"How'd it go?" she asks.

"Good and bad. Good because Mom finally saw what *he* is really like and at last she believes me. He was evil to me and when Mom wouldn't leave with him, he was evil to her too, but you should've seen Miss Tina..." I grin. "She let him have it. She told him that he couldn't be abusive here at Beach Haven."

"Good for her," Josie says.

"Yeah, he was cussing when Mom told him that it was over."

Josie raises her eyebrows at me. "D'you think it's true, is it really over? It took my mom some time to leave my stepfather; they kept breaking up and then getting back together again, and it was only when the police became involved that she was forced to accept that he..."

She goes silent and I don't really know what to say, but I can't just sit here listening to the waves breaking over the sand when there's so much to say.

"Yeah, I think she means it. If you could have seen her when she realized that he'd been lying to her all this time, you'd believe her."

"Good, I'm glad for you," she says, falling silent.

"How do you manage to stop yourself from hating your stepfather after what he did to you?" I ask. "Because I feel so much hatred towards mine, yet what he did to me is loads less than what yours did to you. I feel weighed down with it, like I'm carrying a really heavy backpack on my shoulders. I don't know what to do with it all."

She looks straight into my eyes and I know that she understands me.

"I feel just like that. Sometimes it feels so heavy, as if it's going to bury me."

We fall silent and listen to the seagulls soaring and screeching above us. They don't seem weighed down with feelings of anger and blame; still seagulls don't have stepfathers who molest them, nor do they have stepfathers with messed up pizzas, do they?

Chapter Nine

After dinner we all file into the Group Room and I sit next to Josie because something about her gives me strength.

Miss Tina says, "This afternoon we're going to look at anger and blame, then anger and injustice. What is blame?"

Ollie says, "It's when you hold someone else responsible for something bad that happens; it's someone else's fault."

Alison says, "Yes, but it can be when you make a negative judgment about someone's actions even if you don't have all the facts as to why they behaved as they did."

"Yes, that's right. What's injustice?" Miss Tina asks.

I know what it is but I can't find the words to describe it, but Alison speaks out again and I feel a bit irritated with her; does she know everything?

"It's when something unfair is done to someone that makes them feel bad or oppressed."

"Very good," Miss Tina says, "and does that make you angry?"

"Yes."

"What does your anger make you want to do?"

Alison frowns and then says, "It makes me want to do something to help the person who's being oppressed or hurt."

"So you feel angry when you see an injustice done but you can get rid of your anger by doing something to help change the situation. Okay, now let's look at the anger you feel when you blame someone; what does your anger make you want to do then?"

I think of *him* and so I say, "It makes you want to hurt the person you blame so that they feel as bad as you do."

"So, are you saying that you want to retaliate or get revenge?"

My face suddenly feels hot, and I mumble, "Sometimes."

Miss Tina speaks again, "Anger at the injustices that are done to you is normal but wanting revenge will only hurt you further. If you hang on to blame it will eat you up and stop you growing into the fine people you are all meant to be."

I glance at Josie knowing that she feels the weight of blame on her shoulders just as I do. She should be angry with her stepfather for what he did to her; that was unjust. And although my stepfather didn't molest me, what he did to me was also unjust. If blame ultimately hurts you, how do you get rid of it when you feel so angry inside?

I wonder if I've thought out loud because Miss Tina says, "The only way to stop blame eating you up is to understand everything about what happened, and then find a way to get rid of the anger and pain you feel at the injustice done to you. Sit back and listen to this story which will show you what I mean."

She grins at us. I sit back in my chair and listen.

• • • •

Far, far away in the land that bobbed in and out of view depending upon the sea mist, in a splendid palace beneath a huge mountain, Queen Hension sat dressed in black as her king lay in his grave. The queen's mother, having attended his stately funeral, gathered her bags and the royal carriage was summoned to take her home. As she hugged her tearful daughter she spoke with urgency in her voice, "My child, you have to remarry, for you have no heir. You have to provide your kingdom with a child who will succeed to the throne when you die. Do not wait too long. Find yourself a husband, and soon."

The poor grieving young queen sniffed. The thought of someone replacing her wonderful king was repugnant to her, but she understood her mother's words and nodded, waving as the carriage became a speck in the distance.

Within a few days every fine bachelor in the land had knocked on the great palace door asking to see Queen Hension, and although she received them politely, offering them tea and exquisite little cakes, her mind was elsewhere. Each man, intent on impressing her, boasted about his wealth and strength, but her heart was broken and she longed for her king night after night as her loneliness consumed her.

Deep in the valley beneath the palace lived a young man called Pewmith who lived with his mother, an ambitious and cold-hearted woman. She heard of all the young men calling upon the grieving queen and grabbed Pewmith's arm roughly.

"Get yourself up to the palace and worm your way into Queen Hension's heart. All you have to do is to be sympathetic and let her believe you care. Even you can do that."

Pewmith had been an unhappy child since his father fled in the night, unable to stand his wife's cutting tongue. He had grown up believing that if his father couldn't stand up to his mother, then what chance did he have? And so in order to silence her, Pewmith did as he was told.

The next day Pewmith and his mother set off for the palace, his face grim as she nagged him all the way. As they rang the royal bell she hissed in his ear,

"Now, just remember, be sympathetic and you'll be fine." She spat on her hand and tried to flatten his hair.

They were shown to a regal sitting room where Queen Hension sat forlornly.

Pewmith's mother pushed him sharply in the back and he edged forward as she hung back attempting a deep curtsey. Remembering his mother's words, he coughed nervously and knelt at the young queen's feet.

"I'm so sorry for your loss," he spluttered, gingerly taking her hand.

Queen Hension, used to young men boasting about themselves, looked up in surprise, and as Pewmith smiled at her, so she smiled back.

It happened remarkably quickly, as Pewmith's mother had planned, and they were married within the month. The queen's mother was delighted, hoping for grandchildren who would be heirs to the throne, but as the months turned into years no babies came.

"Why are my prayers left unanswered?" Queen Hension cried to Pewmith, who wrung his hands not knowing what to do or say.

One day while the queen sat in her garden beneath the trees, oblivious to the beauty around her, she pleaded to the gods. "Oh, please send me a child. I beg of you, please, let me have a sweet child to love, one that will be able to rule justly and with kindness over the kingdom when I've gone."

Not all the gods in that land were good—some were fallen gods—and those that heard her plea laughed, deciding to play a trick on her. "Let's grant her wish but give her two identical sons with different hearts and see what happens to the kingdom once they grow up."

They appeared before her and said, "We shall grant you your wish; you shall have twin sons but in return you must call your sons Repré and Compré."

The fallen gods waited and watched with mischief in their hearts.

Queen Hension was beside herself with joy when she gave birth to the identical twin boys, and she stared at the tiny infants believing that the gods had blessed her. But although the two boys looked identical, the fallen gods had given them a challenge that rested in their hearts, unseen by others but that was there nevertheless. It was the way they responded to this challenge that was to make them different.

Queen Hension remembered the names that she had promised to use, and said, "We have to call them Repré and Compré."

Repré and Compré grew up to be fine young princes and Queen Hension believed that nothing could mar her happiness, but little did she suspect that the differences the fallen gods had put in her sons' hearts would one day threaten to destroy them.

It began one morning when Pewmith's mother ar-rived at the palace announcing that she'd come to stay because a fierce wind had destroyed her home. Repré and Compré glanced at each other trying to hide their feelings, for they had always known that their grandmother hated children. They had known what was in their grandmother's heart, as all chil-dren do. Every time she visited she forced them to do all kinds of chores and to walk her dogs around the palace grounds to get the boys out of her way.

Pewmith's mother had only been in the palace for two days when Queen Hension was seen running from the dining room crying, and Pewmith sum-moned Repré and Compré before him saying that a decision had been made about their futures.

"Your grandmother thinks that you should leave the palace for six months to live with different fam-ilies in the kingdom."

Repré and Compré looked shocked and started to speak out but their grandmother shouted over them, dislike on her face.

"You are both spoiled, you have too much. Your mother dotes on you both and has made you weak and spoiled."

Pewmith faltered and shifted uncomfortably, saying, "It's not for very long."

Repré and Compré were very angry and begged their father to reconsider. But when their grand-mother took her walking stick and rapped it sharply on the polished floor, dismissing them with one hand, Pewmith all but ran from the room, ignoring their stricken faces.

They went to find their mother who was still crying into a royal lace handkerchief and began to plead with her.

"Please don't make us go away from the palace, it's not fair. We haven't done anything. Talk to our father and make him change his mind," Repré demanded, and Compré nodded in agreement.

"It is your father's wish," the queen said, looking sad and troubled.

"It's Grandmother's wish, you mean," Repré said bitterly. "Why can't either of you stand up to her? She's a bully."

Queen Hension said nothing, and as Repré and Compré walked out of the palace doors later that day, both were very angry.

"It's not right," Repré said. "We haven't done anything wrong. Why are we being treated this way?"

"I know," Compré said, "I don't understand. Why won't our parents stand up to Grandmother?"

But even though they complained and moaned as the royal carriage rolled through the streets taking them to their new homes, nothing could stop the inevitable from happening.

The driver stopped outside a small tumbled down house and handed Repré a meager suitcase before driving off to deliver Compré to his new home.

That night as the young princes lay in their lumpy beds after a cold shower out in the yard, they longed for the comfort of their own beds and a warm bubble bath in their private bathrooms. Their bellies rumbled with hunger, having been given a stew for dinner that was made almost entirely of potatoes; and as they tossed and turned, nightmares intruded into their sleep of a fine feast upon a golden table dissolving into vile, tasteless gruel.

The next morning Repré cussed under his breath as he was handed an axe and told to chop wood for the fire so that they could cook porridge oats for breakfast. He was cold, hungry and very angry. Compré also had chores to do before he was given any breakfast. He had to clean out the pigsty, collect freshly laid eggs from underneath hens that tried to peck him and made him sneeze when they ruffled their feathers. His back hurt from lying on a lump in his mattress, which smelled as if a cat had marked its territory on it. He felt vaguely sick and wasn't sure if he could stomach breakfast, even though he was very hungry. He, too, was very angry.

The children in the families, jealous of their wealth, stole the princes' clothes so they were forced to wear rags, and within a week both princes had black eyes as the neighborhood children taunted them because their accents were different from their own. Despite both princes writing to their parents, their letters were returned with their grandmother's handwriting on the envelopes saying, "Return to sender, no longer at this address."

A year later news of Pewmith's mother's death spread through the kingdom and the two princes left their meager homes and set off for the palace. Both were hungry and exhausted, skinny and gaunt, and were covered in bruises from being beaten. Both had betrayal resting upon their faces, and anger simmered beneath their relief at being home where they belonged.

Queen Hension threw her arms around her sons, crying at the sight of them. "Your grandmother is dead," she whispered in their ears, "and we are free of her at last." Pewmith faltered when he saw his sons for they turned away from him with anger and contempt in their hearts, blaming him for the hardship they'd been forced to endure.

Night after night Queen Hension wept in her bed as she witnessed the growing hatred that had crept into her sons' hearts towards their father. She prayed to the mountain gods for help, and as she drifted off to sleep one night, the gods whispered in her ear, "There's no blame, only understanding."

When she awoke she knew what to do; she called Repré and Compré to her and began to explain Pewmith's actions to them.

Repré and Compré were instantly angry, their tempers flaring. "Why couldn't he stand up to his mother? She never wanted us around."

Queen Hension looked sad for their words were true; she too had tried and failed to stand up to the woman with hate and greed in her heart, yet she knew that Pewmith had also suffered.

She took their hands and said, "Yes, he should have been stronger against his mother but one of the reasons he did not stop her was that he wanted you both to live amongst the people you will eventually rule. He wanted you to understand those people, their hardships and trials, and although you may have felt hurt, understanding the reasons for his actions must surely help repair your relationship with him."

"He is weak and he had no right," Repré snapped angrily. "Doesn't he know how much he hurt me? Doesn't he know how much pain I endured? It's all his fault; I hate him."

But Compré looked thoughtful and said, "Well, it hurt me a lot, too, but now that you've explained one of the reasons why he did not stop Grandmother from sending us away, I can understand, even though it still hurts. But why didn't you answer our letters?"

Queen Hension looked at the floor with shame written upon her face.

"Your grandmother wouldn't allow us to reply. Your father and I have been weak and your grandmother unjust. I understand why you're angry."

"It's the injustice that makes me so angry," Compré said. *"I'm angry that neither you nor my father stood up to my grandmother's bullying, for she didn't care what happened to us, she just wanted us out of the way."*

Queen Hension nodded with tears in her eyes. "Yes, it's right and proper to be angry when you experience injustice, but understanding the reasons why people behave the way they do surely helps to make the blame go away."

"I don't blame either of you now that I understand the reasons why you all behaved the way you did, even though it still hurts," Compré said.

Repré looked at Compré scornfully, and said, "You're not going to let them get away with it as easily as that, are you, after all the pain and suffering we've endured?"

At that very moment Queen Hension remembered her prayer to the fallen gods, and suddenly she understood why the fallen gods had insisted upon her son's names. She saw the difference the fallen gods had placed in the hearts of her identical sons—Représ heart was full of blame, and Comprés heart was full of understanding. As the realization flowed through her, the princes no longer looked like identical twins. Her heart was filled with pain and she felt tricked and betrayed. She vowed that she would spend the rest of her life trying to rid Repré of the blame that lived in his heart.

One day as Queen Hension strolled around the palace gardens she came upon Compré, who sat slumped as if he had the weight of the world upon his shoulders.

"What troubles you?" she asked him gently.

He smiled with sadness in his eyes and said, "Although I understand why we were sent away, the pain still weighs heavily upon me. What can I do to rid myself of it for I do not want blame to begin to eat away at me?"

Queen Hension thought for a moment and, knowing the weight of pain, thought how she could help her sons.

"I know," she said, "we'll go on a journey up the mountain. Put your walking boots on and find a backpack. Go and fetch Repré, for he must come too."

Repré muttered angrily as they began to climb the mountain, and as they stumbled across loose rocks underfoot, Queen Hension told the princes to put them in their backpacks. The princes looked confused but did as they were asked. By the time they reached the top of the mountain their backpacks were full to the brim with rocks that weighed heavily on their shoulders; the straps cut into them causing them pain. They longed to take the backpacks off but Queen Hension would not allow them to. Confusion rested on their faces.

"My beautiful sons, I know you were hurt, but what you do with that hurt will determine whether

you will be weighed down with blame forever. See each rock in your backpack as the pain you feel. Reach into it and throw them off the mountain. Free yourselves of the pain that fosters blame."

They slung their backpacks over one shoulder and began throwing the heavy rocks one by one as far as they could, listening to them crash on the boulders far below them. Gradually, as their backpacks were emptied, the pain on their shoulders eased and Compré smiled at his mother.

"That feels so much better," he said. "I have thrown my pain away, and I don't feel weighed down anymore."

But Repré scoffed at his brother, and even though his backpack was empty and the pain eating into his shoulders relieved, the blame that lived in his heart remained.

As the months went by he became more and more eaten up with blame, and as his anger grew, his heart began to shrivel with hatred. Not only did he hate his father, his dead grandmother and all the people who had hurt him during his year away from the palace, but now as Compré s heart grew with understanding and compassion, Repré began to hate Compré, too.

The fallen gods laughed as they watched Repré being destroyed by the blame in his heart, and Queen Hension's heart slowly broke as she watched him gradually shrivel and die.

Years later Queen Hension died and Compré became king—King Comprehension. Although he occasionally still felt the remnants of hurt in his heart, he used the painful experiences that he had endured during those twelve months he'd been cast aside to understand his people. He was able to rule the people of his kingdom with understanding and compassion. He was the finest king that ever lived, and the fallen gods stopped laughing, their mischief having been beaten by understanding."

• • • •

Miss Tina looks at us, and says, "Do you understand? Being angry at injustices done to you is natural but it's what you do with your anger that matters. If you choose to hang on to your anger and blame, it will prevent you from growing as a person, and you will be damaged by your anger. Both the princes' parents were weak and should have stood up for them against their evil grandmother, but in the end both boys had a choice as to what to do. You'll notice that they were both hurt by their parents' actions but after they understood why their parents acted as they had, it was Repré who chose to hang on to his blame, which then fed his anger. He failed to grow as a person, and began to hate everyone until his heart shriveled and died."

Everyone's quiet until Josie speaks.

"Are you telling me that by understanding why my stepfather molested me, I won't blame him?"

She sounds incredulous and Miss Tina smiles at her.

"My dear, no amount of understanding in such an awful case of injustice towards a child will completely get rid of the anger you so rightly feel, but the whole point is to learn how to prevent it from shriveling your heart and completely ruining your life. You can understand why your mother took so long to believe you," I glance at Josie and give her a bleak smile as I think of my own mom not believing me, "and then you can learn ways to get rid of the pain, so that you are not eaten up by blame."

"But how?" Josie asks. "It all weighs heavily upon me, too, like the two princes. I don't want it to, but it does."

"Think of how much energy a person uses being angry; well, it takes a lot more energy to remain angry. If you can channel that energy you can use it to fight injustice, and you'll grow into a person who'll make the world a better place. But if you are unable to let go of the anger and hurt you feel when some injustice has been done to you, you'll be eaten up by the desire to get revenge, and to make others hurt as much as you hurt. Your negative feelings will be damaging to you and they will shrivel your heart; you'll never find peace of mind and no one will want to be around you. That's the bottom line. You may feel that your anger and blame are justified, but ultimately you will become the type of person that no one will want to be with."

We're all quiet and I'm deep in thought. Am I going to be Repré, eaten up with hatred and anger towards *him* for what he did to my mom and me? Will my heart shrivel and die? I hope not. Yes, I feel angry towards him, and if I'm honest I have to admit that right this minute I hate him, but if I try to understand everything that's happened maybe I'll be like Compré. I'll grow and my heart won't be shriveled and bitter.

Miss Tina looks at me and smiles.

"Shane, you had a difficult morning. It was obvious that injustice has been done to you, and you have every right to feel angry. How will you deal with your anger so that it doesn't hurt you further?"

I think for a moment and then I remember the pictures Miss Tina makes come into my head.

"When you talked about *his* pizza being messed up, that helped me to understand."

"Good."

"Yes, but I still feel really angry towards him and..." I look down at the floor, "...and I hate him. How do I get rid of those feelings?"

"You didn't add 'pain' to your list of feelings," Miss Tina said.

I look up at her. Does she know *everything* that's inside me?

Chapter Ten

The next morning I wake up bathed in sweat, my heart hammering, as images of *him*, dressed as a fallen god laughing at me trying to carry a pile of rocks, dissolve from my mind. As my heart begins to slow, I lie still and listen to the waves crashing on the shore. Today feels like a new beginning. This time yesterday my mom was still with *him*. I wonder how it's going to be from now on. Will we stay in the same house or move, and if we move will I have to go to a different school? School...I haven't even thought of school since I was suspended for terroristic threatening. Will they allow me back? How will the other kids act towards me if they do?

I can't believe that my life could change so much in such a short time. A year ago everything was fine. I was making good grades and a member of all sorts of clubs. Mom said I had a great future ahead of me;

yeah, but that was before I went to jail and got myself a criminal record. What's going to happen to me now that I've messed things up?

I turn over and will sleep to come upon me again, but as images of *him* dressed as a fallen god laughing at me threaten to creep into my mind, I get up and head for the shower.

As I scrub myself under the hot jets of water, I wonder if there is such a thing as Sadness Beads and Sadness Slime.

Josie sits next to me at breakfast.

"What's up?" she asks.

I'm beginning to really like her for she seems to know where I'm at without me saying anything.

"Oh, not much."

She pulls a face that says she doesn't believe me, and I smile.

"Oh, it's nothing really. I just feel that I've messed my life up and I don't know if I can get it back on track. If *he's* really gone, then life at home will be much better but what do I do about everything I've screwed up at school?"

Ollie sits down next to us.

"What's up?"

I don't feel like saying it all over again. Josie speaks for me.

"He feels like he's messed things up and doesn't know how to put them right."

"What things?" he asks me.

I think for a minute as it all seems a bit over-whelming, and then I say, "Everything."

But Josie chips in, "No, Shane, not everything. Now that your stepfather's gone, things at home will be fine. It sounds to me like the main thing you're worried about is school."

"I suppose it is."

"What about school?" Ollie asks.

"Whether they'll have me back, and whether I can catch up with all the work I've missed," I say miserably. "I don't know how the other kids will be to-wards me, either. Will my friends still want to know me when I get back?"

Josie looks affronted. "Well, if they don't, then they aren't the sort of friends you need,"

"Listen," Ollie says, "I've been suspended from school before and it was no big deal going back. Yeah, if the teachers think you're going to cause more trouble they'll watch you, and that doesn't feel very nice, but as soon as they see you're not going to be a problem, they'll let up. And like Josie says, if your friends don't want to know you, then they aren't really your friends. As for any work you've missed, you can make it up. Just go and see your teacher and counselor; they'll help you. Don't worry about it. If they can see that you're really serious about getting things back on track, they'll help you. That's what they're there for, that's their job."

He grins at me and punches my arm as he gets up to take his plate to the kitchen.

"C'mon," Josie says, getting up, "It's time for group."

Miss Tina is already sitting in her chair waiting for us and gradually as everyone sits down we become quiet.

She smiles at us and, just as she opens her mouth to speak, the door opens. We all look towards it and see Ken struggling through the door carrying a big box with his chin perched on the top. Wayne and Ollie jump up to help him.

"Thanks, Ken. No problems then?" Miss Tina asks.

Ken laughs and says, "Nope, they just asked if I was going on vacation."

I don't know what they're talking about until Miss Tina opens the box.

"Yesterday we talked about injustice, anger and pain, and the story showed how Repré and Compré dealt differently with their anger, their pain and with the injustice done to them. Repré hung on to his anger and blame refusing to let it go, and it destroyed him in the end. But although Compré felt as much anger and blame to begin with, he tried to understand everything that had led to the injustice happening to him. When he did understand, the only thing he then had to deal with was the pain he felt."

My face feels a bit hot as I remember that Miss Tina corrected me yesterday saying that I'd forgotten to add "pain" to my list of feelings.

"Pain is a natural human feeling, although I'm sure that at times we all wish it weren't, because it hurts, but feeling pain is what makes us human. The best way to deal with emotional pain is to allow yourself to cry. The human body can only really cry for a short amount of time before the brain produces chemicals that make you feel better. Once that happens, it's useful to do something symbolic with your pain, because it makes you feel like you've gained control of it, and you are not being controlled by it. By doing something symbolic with your feelings you empower yourself, and after having suffered an injustice being done to you, which makes you feel powerless, it's very important for your recovery that you feel empowered and in control again."

She starts to open the box in front of her, and I can't help but grin as she pulls out loads of backpacks.

She smiles at us.

"So...today we're going to do something symbolic to help you get rid of your pain. Each of you is going to spend the morning walking along the beach picking up rocks, just as Repré and Compré did. As you put each rock into the backpack you are to say which feeling it represents. Continue collecting rocks until your backpacks are full and you feel the weight of your pain cutting into your shoulders. Then, bring them back into the Group Room and leave them by your chairs, and we'll talk about it after lunch. Okay?"

Josie smiles at me as we each pick up a backpack from the heap on the floor.

It's a beautiful day and the sun sparkles on the moving ocean, blinding me. I put my shades on and begin to walk, my feet slipping on the dry, powdery sand.

"Let's walk on the wet sand," Josie says, nodding towards the ocean. "It's easier, and there are more rocks, too."

We wander off, the others drifting away in other directions, all scanning the shore for rocks. There's seaweed strewn across the wet sand and it moves as the waves roll back and forth.

We take turns in picking up the stray rocks.

"This rock is the anger I felt when *he* got me into trouble," I say, trying to do as Miss Tina asked, even though I feel a bit silly.

Josie picks up a rock and frowns, thinking.

"This rock represents my pain at what *he* did to me," and she slams it into the backpack, her face grim.

"This rock is the blame I feel towards my mom for not waiting to get married until she really knew him," I say, and throw it into my backpack with the same anger I saw flashing upon Josie's face. My heart's racing as I think about all the things that make me angry and cause me pain, and for the blame that eats me up.

We stoop to pick up a rock and name it to each other in turn, and when there seem to be no more, we head towards the white cliffs, where chalk rocks lie scattered about. The sun's beating down on us and Josie holds up a rock that looks like a head.

"This rock represents *his* head," and picking up another she says, "and this rock is *his* foul mouth. They represent my anger at him kissing me."

She looks so hurt and I realize that although I've felt pain in my life, it's nothing compared to what she's felt. My thoughts don't take my pain away, but they do give me something to hang on to, something that actually makes me feel a bit thankful. I put my hand on her arm.

"Are you all right?"

She grits her teeth and hisses through them.

"Yes, I won't let him beat me, even though it hurts."

Her determination makes me feel admiration for her.

I pick up a rock and I want to match her honesty, so I hold it in front of me, and say, "This rock is the pain I felt when my mom chose *him* over me." I feel raw, having stated the one thing I've been avoiding. I was jealous when she brought *him* into our lives, I felt pushed aside. My face is burning but Josie seems to rescue me. She smiles at me.

"This rock is the blame I feel towards my mom for not protecting me."

"This rock is my anger towards my mom for never listening to me."

"This rock is the pain I feel because I miss my dad." She dumps a big rock into her backpack.

"This is the pain I felt when *he* laughed at me behind my mom's back."

"This is the pain I felt when my mom refused to believe me."

"This is my anger at being sent to juvenile detention," I say feeling suddenly chilled despite the sun on my back.

We stand there beneath the cliffs naming each rock with all the anger, blame and pain we've ever felt until our backpacks are full. They are so heavy that we have to help each other load them onto our backs, and I have to squat down so that Josie can help me.

As we walk back to Beach Haven, the backpack straps cut into my shoulders, and I can see Josie flinching, too. My face is red by the time we get to the Group Room.

Miss Tina says, "Is your bag of pain heavy?"

"Very."

She helps us pull them off and asks to see our shoulders. There are bright red marks and deep indentations where the weight of the backpacks has been.

I rub my shoulders trying to ease the pain, but all through lunch they still hurt. All the kids are sitting around complaining of the pain in their shoulders.

Later when we're in group, Miss Tina asks us how it felt carrying our pain around.

"It hurt like crazy," Ollie says. "When the bag was full it was really painful and you couldn't forget that it was there, either."

"So holding on to your pain, anger and blame causes you further pain," Miss Tina points out, "and keeps you focused on it."

"Yeah," he grins, pulling his tee-shirt off his shoulders to show us the red marks that refuse to fade. "There was a lot of pain in my bag."

"How did it feel when you named your feelings? Josie, how did you feel?"

"I don't know," she says frowning. "I suppose it forced me to think of what each rock represented... they weren't just rocks anymore, but thinking about what they represented also brought those feelings back, so it was hard."

"Did anyone else feel that way?" Miss Tina asks.

"Yeah, I did," I say. "Saying what each rock represented brought all the feelings back to me again."

"In order for this symbolic exercise to work, the rocks can't just remain rocks," Miss Tina says. "They have to really take on the feeling they represent, because when you throw them away, like Repré and Compré were asked to do, the symbolic act of throwing them away will only allow you to get rid of your pain if the rocks mean something."

Alison looks thoughtful. "When Queen Hension asked Repré and Compré to throw their pain away by throwing the rocks from the mountain top, did it work for Compré because he was able to visualize the rock being his anger, blame and pain? Could it be that Repré wasn't able or willing to let the rocks represent his feelings?"

She looks as if she's thinking to herself yet talking out loud.

"Maybe," Miss Tina answered, looking pleased with Alison for thinking it through. "Perhaps Repré refused to try and imagine the rocks to be his feelings because for some reason he didn't want to let go of them. Perhaps he wasn't ready."

"Yeah, but why would someone want to hang on to feelings that hurt them?" Wayne asks, frowning.

"Well, that's a difficult question," Miss Tina says, as we all watch her, waiting for the answer. "Sometimes it's easier for people to stick with their anger, blame and pain instead of working through them. By refusing to work through their feelings, they think they'll avoid reliving the pain. They also avoid exploring their own behavior. Sometimes it just feels too scary to work through the pain, but whatever the reason, holding on to pain, anger and blame will weigh heavily upon you and will hurt you further."

I think as she's talking. I don't want to think about *him* and the pain he caused me, but neither do I want to be weighed down by it either.

"When you feel ready to get rid of the pain that weighs you down, wear your backpack down to the beach to remind yourself of how heavy it feels. Then throw each rock as far as you can out into the sea and watch it sink to the bottom, to be gone forever. You can say what each rock represents to you as you throw it away, if that helps. You'll find that the physical act of throwing something heavy will help you to feel that you have actually thrown your pain away. I don't want you to do this until you feel ready, though. Don't do it because you think you should, and don't do it just because your peers may be able to. It has to be when *you* feel ready to leave your pain behind and get on with your life without it.

"When you've thrown all the rocks into the sea, I want you to put the backpack back on again to let you feel that the heaviness has gone, and how light it feels once you've gotten rid of your pain. Walk along the shore to really feel the difference. You can wear your empty backpack for as long as you like in order to remind you that you *chose* to get rid of your pain."

Miss Tina stands up and says, "It's a beautiful day and you've all got a lot to think about, so have the rest of the day off. See you later."

We all file out of the Group Room to get a soda and I'm just about to go outside to sit on the beach when Ken calls me.

"Hey, Shane, you've got a visitor."

I follow him to reception and my stomach does a double flip. Standing there is the big black prison guard that saved me in the shower. I don't know what to say, but he moves towards me and puts out his hand.

"Hi Shane, how're you doing?"

"Fine," I mumble.

Ken sees my discomfort and says, "Shane, why don't you take..."

"Brent," the guard says.

"Why don't you take Brent for a walk along the beach."

I head for the door feeling awkward, not knowing what to say, and it's several minutes before he speaks to me.

"So you're okay, are you? I've been worried about you. I see kids like you all the time. The first time they find themselves in detention it's a shock and they have to act tough to survive. Each time they come back to jail, that tough act sticks with them and they can lose who they once were. It saddens me."

I look at him, surprised to hear him speak that way.

"You're lucky that you've been given the opportunity to come here and work on your problems before your 'tough act' robbed you of who you really are. How's it going? I hear that it can be pretty tough here too, but in a different way."

At last he gives me something that I can answer.

"I'm doing fine, and yeah, it is tough. You have to be really honest with yourself and with everyone else; there's no hiding place. You can't kid yourself here."

"That's good. So what are you going to do when you leave here?"

"I don't know. I've messed things up. My mom said I had a good future ahead of me, but now that I've gotten myself into trouble I've blown it."

"Let's sit," Brent says, and drops down onto the warm sand. "Listen, when I was your age life was tough, very tough, and I started to run with the wrong crowd. I didn't see that I had a choice; it was tough on the streets. Anyway, I got into trouble and ended up in detention several times. And each time I was locked up the tougher I tried to be, until I almost forgot who I really was."

I glance at him.

"It was only when I saw my uncle end up in jail for life that I started to think about where I was heading. It was hard because everyone I knew acted tough and didn't know what to do with their lives. It was almost as if they thought that they had no future because they'd messed up, but you know, that's not true."

"Isn't it?" I ask, because that's what's worrying me. Have I got a future even though I've been in jail?

"No, it's not. Just because you made a mistake

doesn't mean that you can't pick yourself up and carry on. You can even use the experience to help others."

"How?"

"Well, after I'd been in juvenile detention several times, I was lucky—a youth worker took an interest in me and helped me finish school. He spent hours with me trying to get me to drop my tough act and to be who I really am. He made me see that because of everything I'd experienced, I would know, really know, how it feels in here." He thumps his chest. "You see, because I really knew how it felt to be locked up and to be afraid and feel hurt, I'd be able to help kids when they were hurt and afraid. He helped me to see that I could make something of myself and use those rough times to help others. He helped me to get into college to become a social worker."

"I thought you were a prison guard," I say, feeling confused.

"Well, I guess I am, sometimes. I work at the detention center to help pay my way through college, and to work with the kids."

I don't say anything but deep inside me I'm glad he works there, and very glad that he was there when I was in the shower.

"Anyway, the point is, don't let one mistake make you think that you can't have a good future. Your whole life's ahead of you and you can turn it around. I'll do anything I can to help you, just name it. Y'know, when someone helps you in life, it's a great thing to be able to pass that on and help someone else."

He stands up and brushes the sand from his jeans.

I don't know what to say so I mumble, "Thanks," as he reaches into his pocket.

"Here's my card. Call me if you need anything, all right? Promise?"

"Yeah, thanks."

He walks away and I watch him leave as Josie walks over to me and sits down.

"Who was that?"

I tell her what he said, and she agrees with him.

"See, I told you that it'll be all right. You've just got to want it to be okay. Are you going to call him when you leave here?"

I think for a minute, staring out to sea. My mom said that she married *him* in order for me to have a man in my life. She obviously thought I needed one, so perhaps I do. If I take Brent up on his offer, I can have a man in my life without her ever feeling the need to provide one for me.

"Yeah, I think I will. He seems all right."

She smiles at me and I feel my face burn.

Later, I stare at the television, realizing that I haven't taken in one single word; my mind is elsewhere. I leave the other kids and slip out onto the playground, watching the sun sinking down towards the horizon over the ocean. My head seems to be full of thoughts and I feel weighed down by them. As the words "weighed down" flash into my mind, I think about my backpack full of "pain rocks" sitting by my chair in the Group Room, and suddenly I know what I want to do. I want to feel light, I want to feel free, I want to get rid of everything to do with *him*. I never want to feel angry about *him* anymore, and I want to be free from the blame that keeps my pain alive.

I jump up like a man with a mission and head towards the Group Room.

"Wait up," Josie cries. "Where are you going? Are you okay?"

"Yeah, I'm fine. Never felt better. I'm ready to throw my 'pain rocks' away."

"D'you want me to come with you?"

I look at her and suddenly there's nothing I'd like better.

"Yeah, if you want to."

She helps me put the heavy backpack on and immediately I can feel it biting into my shoulders.

"Imagine having to carry this much pain around with you everyday of your life," I say, trying to shift the backpack a bit to ease my shoulders, but nothing helps; it hurts. "C'mon then, let's go."

By the time we reach the edge of the shore my shoulders are killing me, and it's a relief to haul the backpack off and put it on the sand. The sun has almost gone, leaving long shadows stretching from our feet.

"Right," I say, as I reach into the bag and pull out a large rock. "This rock represents the pain I feel that my real dad left me," and with as much force as I can muster I hurl it as far as I can into the ocean. We watch it arch across the waves that roll up the shore and plop heavily into the water.

"Yeah!"

I reach for another.

"This rock represents the pain I felt when *he* ridiculed me." This time I throw the rock with such force that it lands even further away.

"Wow," Josie says, grinning.

"This rock is the pain I felt when my mom didn't stick up for me when *he* picked on me."

With each rock I pick up, I name the pain it represents and throw it as far away into the ocean as my strength will allow me. When the bag is empty, I feel exhausted.

Josie is laughing at the determination on my face and suddenly I feel light and happy. I flop onto the sand and I can't seem to stop myself from laughing. I feel amazing. I feel free. Now I know how Compré felt after throwing all his rocks off the mountain, and I know deep down that since I've been able to throw my "pain rocks" away, I won't be eaten up with blame and anger, as Repré was.

"C'mon," Josie says, getting up. "You've got to

walk along the beach to remind yourself how light you feel now that you've gotten rid of your pain."

I slip my arms into the straps of the bag, and it feels so light as it settles on my shoulders, almost as if it isn't there. As I start to walk along the shore, Josie slips her hand into mine, beaming at me, and I don't want this moment to ever end.

About the Author

Dr. Celia Banting earned her Ph.D. by studying suicide attempts in adolescents and developing a risk assessment tool to identify those young people who may be at risk of attempting suicide. She identified several risk factors which, when combined, could increase the likelihood of an individual attempting suicide. Rather than write "how to" books or text books to help teenagers cope with the risk factors, Dr. Banting has incorporated therapeutic interventions into novels that adolescents will be able to identify with. These novels are designed to increase the adolescents' ability to take care of themselves, should they have minimal support in their families.

Dr. Banting's career has revolved around caring for children in a variety of settings in both the United Kingdom and the United States. She is dedicated to helping troubled children avoid the extreme act of suicide.

WIGHITA PRESS ORDER FORM

Book Title	Price	Qty.	Total

I Only Said I Had No Choice
ISBN 0-9786648-0-9 $14.99   x ____ $_____
> Shane learns how to control his anger and make positive life
> choices; and he gains understanding about adult co-dependency.

I Only Said "Yes" So That They'd Like Me
ISBN 0-9786648-1-7 $14.99   x ____ $_____
> Melody learns how to cope with being bullied by the in-crowd at
> school and explores the emotional consequences of casual sex.
> She raises her self-esteem and learns what true beauty is.

I Only Said I Couldn't Cope
ISBN 0-9786648-2-5 $14.99   x ____ $_____
> Adam learns how to deal with grief and depression. He works
> through the grieving process and explores his perceptions of
> death and life.

I Only Said I Didn't Want You Because I Was Terrified
ISBN 0-9786648-3-3 $14.99   x ____ $_____
> Hannah experiences peer pressure to drink alcohol. She learns
> about teenage pregnancy, birth, and caring for a new baby.
> Hannah faces the consequences of telling lies and learns how to
> repair broken trust.

I Only Said I Was Telling the Truth
ISBN 0-9786648-4-1 $14.99   x ____ $_____
> Ruby embarks upon a journey to rid herself of the damaging
> emotional consequences of sexual abuse.

Sub Total $_____

Sales Tax 7.5% ($1.13 per book) $_____

Shipping/handling $_____
1st book, $2.50; each add'l. book $1.00 / U.S. orders only.
(For orders outside the United States, contact Wighita Press.)

TOTAL DUE $_____

PLEASE PRINT ALL INFORMATION.

Customer name: _____

Mailing address: _____

City/State/Zip: _____

Phone Number(s): _____

E-mail address: _____

**Make check or money order payable to Wighita Press and
mail order to:** P.O. Box 30399, Little Rock, Arkansas 72260-0399
Look for us on the web at: www.wighitapress.com   (501) 455-0905